# Dale Mayer

# TERK'S GUARDIANS
## MORRISON 13

MORRISON: TERK'S GUARDIANS, BOOK 13
Beverly Dale Mayer
Valley Publishing Ltd.



ISBN-13: 978-1-778866-55-5
Print Edition

## Books in This Series:

Radar, Book 1

Legend, Book 2

Bojan, Book 3

Langdon, Book 4

Walker, Book 5

Reid, Book 6

Sanders, Book 7

Nate, Book 8

Royal, Book 9

Alex, Book 10

Royce, Book 11

Trevor, Book 12

Morrison, Book 13

Wallace, Book 14

## About This Book

Morrison had been shadowing the jewel thieves, searching for a pattern... a motive... something beyond mere greed. His instincts whispered of a bigger scheme lurking behind these heists, yet uncovering it was proving more elusive than he had anticipated. He was always a step behind, chasing shadows, until fate finally dealt him a card he could play.

Sadie was in the bank, lost in her routine transactions, when chaos erupted. The robbery was terrifying enough, but a chilling familiarity about one of the masked figures sent shivers down her spine. Her heart ached at the thought, but silence was not an option, especially when the stakes were this high...

Thrown together by circumstance, Morrison and Sadie form a fragile alliance, one fraught with tension and unspoken attraction. As they delve deeper, the lines between family and foe blur, and their quest to prevent another nightmare becomes as much about trust and betrayal as it is about stopping the thieves.

**Sign up to be notified of all Dale's releases here!**

https://geni.us/DaleNews

# PROLOGUE

THE NEXT MORNING Terk sat at his breakfast table, the gang in front of him, and smiled. "Looks like we got that one beat too," he said, with a smile.

Celia nodded. She was looking a little tired. He gently pulled a lock of hair off her cheek, and she smiled. "I'm fine. It's just the babies keeping me up."

He nodded, knowing full well what a toll the babies took on her, and yet what quiet joy she took in working with them on a constant basis.

At the same moment, Damon walked in.

Terk smiled at him and said, "Sounds like a job well done."

"A job well done, indeed, but it was a bit dicey there for a while. Once you get lawyers involved, it can get pretty ugly."

Terk laughed. "Isn't that the truth? We have plenty of lawyers that we're dealing with in our way too."

"Problems?" Damon asked.

"No, not at all, just setting up all the business stuff that still needs to be done," Terk replied, waving his hand about.

"And, speaking of all that, where's Riff?" Damon asked in a curious tone. "I didn't see him on this job at all. Usually he has a habit of popping in and out, like a bad penny."

"Usually he does. He got another lead on his fiancée's

murder," Terk replied. "So he's off on that again."

"One of these days," Sophia interjected, from the far end of the table, "we must have something solid to go on to help him out."

"We're still looking," Terk muttered in a dark tone. "Aren't you?"

"I am. We all are. When we're not on jobs, we all pitch in, looking to see what we can find for him. There's just … not much there."

Terk nodded. "We will find something eventually. However, with Angela back and forth, looking after babies," he added, with a laugh, "it's not as if we get a chance to avoid *that* issue."

Sophia nodded. "Those two are an interesting couple. Yet they're rarely ever here at the same time."

"I'm pretty sure that's by choice," Celia shared. "You and I both know something is between them, something that's unfinished and that needs a resolution on this murder case first, before they have any chance of going forward with a healthy relationship."

"And both would tell you right off the bat," Damon shared, with a wry smile, "that neither of them wants to move forward with anything that involves the other. … We all know that would be a lie. At least not so much of a lie as just not acknowledging what's in front of them. Mostly I think out of loyalty to his dead fiancée—equally for both of them."

"Isn't it great how we get ourselves all twisted up on things like that?" Lorelei pointed out, as she waddled in, with her massive belly.

Terk shook his head and said, "I presume Angela's popping in soon, with your due date approaching."

"She should be," Lorelei said, with a laugh. "Hey, that's the way it works between doctor and patient."

Terk nodded. "At least she's here when we need her, and, when we don't, we know everything's good." He looked around and noted, "Not sure we have any more jobs at the moment. I think we should all enjoy a few days' worth of a well-earned rest."

"The minute you say that," Wade declared, as he walked in and sat down, "it's almost an invitation for trouble."

"It is, indeed," Terk agreed, with a laugh.

When Jonas phoned just a few moments later, Terk sighed. "I never should have mentioned taking any days off." He answered the phone on the second ring. "What's up, Jonas?"

"The government wants to thank you for your service," he began, with an ironic tone.

Terk laughed at that. "Glad to hear it. Still, I can't imagine that's all you are calling about."

"Regardless, I'm pretty sure that this is a good partnership," he said.

"Yeah, we were just talking about the fact that we don't have a job on our list at the moment."

Jonas snorted at that. "Don't look at me. I'm trying to take some time off. Although … I did pass your name on to another department."

"Yeah? What department is that?"

"MI5," he said quietly. "Something homegrown has soured."

"Soured how?" Terk asked, raising an eyebrow and looking around at everybody.

"In this case it's jewel thieves. The last group, a team of four, went in, took everybody hostage, shot up the security guard and the store manager, grabbed everything inside the shop, and then disappeared. They've done this three times now."

"Why is MI5 interested?"

"Because it's been linked to a local terrorist group," Jonas explained. "I don't know whether that's just a cover or a convenient smokescreen. However, I did tell MI5 that they may very well contact you, if they need a hand and want to get the case locked down. Of course that doesn't mean they believe me."

"Not sure I want to work for somebody who doesn't really see the value in our work either," Terk replied.

"Don't be so stuffy. If they haven't worked with you, they don't know what you can do. The head guy knows a little bit, and he knows that your track record is pretty special."

"Is there anybody local in particular working on this?"

"He's got, … jeez, who is it now? … Morrison Hadley. Yeah, his name's Morrison, and he has been tracking them for quite a while. He possibly has an inside line now on something because the sister of one of the security guards was actually on the scene at the time of the shooting, and she said she recognized one of the crew."

"So then why do they need me?" Terk asked, frowning at his team members gathered around the table. "If he's already got an inside line …"

"I think more or less because the sister said something about *This is a Terk job*. When Morrison relayed that to me, I presumed that this guy or the whole group—or team or whatever you want to call these people—I gather they have abilities."

"Well, shit," Terk grumbled. "That's not good."

"Exactly," Jonas said, "which is one of the reasons why I thought maybe you needed a heads-up." He added almost apologetically, "I know Morrison's good. I just don't know if he's *your* kind of good. I don't know if he's got any of *your kind* of gifts," he shared, with emphasis. "Yet the guard's sister was pretty adamant."

"You have a name for the sister?"

"Yeah, Sadie," he said, "Sadie Templeton."

"Good, in that case I'll be in touch with them."

And, with that, Jonas signed off.

Terk announced to the others, "This one could get ugly."

The team nodded in unison.

"But, if we've got people with abilities doing high-end jewelry robberies and shooting people," Wade noted, "you know we have to go after them."

Terk nodded. "At least we're in agreement on that."

Just then his phone lit up. He looked down and shared, "MI5 calling. You guys ready for this?"

They all nodded. "Absolutely."

"Here we go." Terk put it on Speakerphone.

# CHAPTER 1

MORRISON SHIFTED IN his vehicle, the front seat uncomfortable, as he studied the jewelry store. He'd been at it since five this morning, watching to see what happened, who was around, and just checking out the general area. He didn't know for sure that this would be the next place where the jewel thieves would strike, but his instincts, his senses, … insisted. He kept coming back here, not even sure how it was connected to his current cases.

A little nudge inside him forewarned that maybe the heist crew were also casing out this same location.

So he opened his senses wider to see if he caught the energy of someone nearby.

Still nothing. Yet he knew this place was under surveillance. And this heist crew may even have abilities—which meant, for all he knew, they could be in the ethers right now, staring down at him. With a shake of his head, he muttered, "This case will be a bigger mess than expected."

He checked his phone for the time, as he was supposed to meet Sadie in two hours. From his current intel, she was a witness to the robbery, the sister of a guard at one of the three latest jewelry store hits. Sadie may have recognized something about one of the members of this jewelry heist gang. Yet as soon as Morrison woke this morning, he found himself right back here at this jewelry store, a potential for the robbers, so Morrison continued to look for answers.

The fact that this location hadn't been hit yet was interesting because it was one of the largest jewelry stores in town, so why not? It did have state-of-the-art security, and it was certainly one of the higher-end places, a step above the jewelry stores the gang had been hitting recently, but that didn't give this store a free pass. Morrison suspected that the robbers were just working their way up to it, as if the other robberies were just building up to this one, which might be a real haul.

It was Morrison's job and his passion to stop them before they had a chance. The fact that they were killing as they ran rampant made it doubly important to stop them as fast as he could.

He shifted again in his car seat, watching the area while opening his senses wider, waiting for something, anything that would tell him what the hell this group was up to. The fact that he couldn't get anything was all the more disturbing because it made him fear the thieves had actual knowledge as to how energy worked, as if they had found a way to somehow—he didn't want to say *camouflage their steps*—but they remained slippery, maybe due to some extra skills that he didn't want the bad guys to have, for sure.

He now felt also this fated sense of waiting, this sense of a shift in the energy around him that something was about to blow. Not today, maybe not even tomorrow, but soon. His senses were screaming that it had to do with this jewelry store, that this jewelry store in particular wanted to be at the heart of it. He stayed for several more minutes, but nothing was happening here.

Finally he turned on his engine and pulled away from the curb, checking the mirrors to see if anybody watched him as he left, and again found nothing. The place was dead. It was only six in the morning after all, yet he couldn't quite escape that feeling of someone watching him.

As he drove toward the restaurant, his phone rang. He glanced down at it and frowned, not recognizing the number. Yet he still answered it. The voice that came through the phone was not one he expected. "Levi?" he asked in astonishment.

Levi laughed. "Yeah, it's me," he replied pleasantly.

"What the hell, and how did you get my number?"

"Let's just say it's been passed through a few departments."

"Son of a bitch. It shouldn't have been passed at all," he muttered, still in shock as he listened to his old friend. "What the hell happened to you? I heard you and Ice finally got married."

"Married and reproducing, … like rabbits apparently," he added. "It's all good. We've got three, and that's more than enough, right?"

"Good God," he murmured. "You know that's not something I ever saw coming in your life."

"Yeah, I didn't see it coming either." Levi chuckled. "And I should have. I mean, I really should have, but, hey, life has been fairly challenging for the last few years, but it's been good."

"I'm glad to hear it," Morrison said, as he cautiously drove toward the restaurant. "Yet I'm guessing you didn't call just to catch up, so what's up?"

"I'm sure you'll understand fairly quickly," he muttered. "Remember Merk?"

"Sure, I do. He's kind of unforgettable. What about him? Still a tough badass like always, I assume," he added with a hint of laughter.

"Pretty much. He's also married and has kids too, twins."

"Good God." At that, he pulled off to the side of the road and stared at the phone. "I'm struggling with this whole *homespun family bliss* thing."

"Yeah, we all took the plunge and still can't quite believe it happened. One by one we found partners, then life changed in a big way for all of us," he shared. "Now it seems to be the most natural thing in the world."

"That's all good for you guys, but you haven't got me convinced, that's for sure," he muttered.

"Meaning you're still single?"

"Do you really have to ask? Who the hell would take an old reprobate like me?"

At that, Levi snorted. "We all thought the same thing too."

"Oh hell, you always had Ice," he muttered. "She was always there, looking after you, watching your back, flying you in and out of trouble."

"I know," Levi agreed, his voice thickening with emotion. "Believe me that I know just how lucky I am."

"Yeah, she never spent a single minute looking at the rest of us."

"I finally married her, and she's quite content right now."

"Are you sure?" he teased. "You never know. Maybe she's had a little too much domestic tranquility, and somebody needs to come in and shake up your lives a little."

Levi burst out laughing. "I think all of us wouldn't mind if it calmed down around here," he admitted, still chuckling. "We've got a lot going on in our world. Lots of marriages, lots of babies, and plenty of work. It's all good though. I'm sure no one else could have managed any better than we've done for ourselves."

"So, that's all good, but it brings me back to my original question. Why have you called me?"

"So, Merk has a twin brother."

"Terkel?"

"Yeah, that's him."

"That's one scary dude." Morrison smiled because he did know Terk, at least a little, but still, Morrison remained uncertain as to what Terk could actually do.

Levi muttered, "In one way, yes, Terk's one scary dude, but he saved our backs time and time again."

"I don't know him that well, so I doubt he's into saving my ass."

"No, but MI6 has passed his name to MI5, apparently related to somebody you are due to meet this morning."

He shook his head. "Good God," he muttered, "how the hell did this come around to this morning's appointment?"

"She mentioned the name Terk, and that immediately triggers all kinds of other issues," Levi noted.

"And, of course, nobody told me that."

"I'm telling you now," Levi stated, his voice cheerful on the phone. "And expect to hear from Terk sometime soon."

"So, whether I like it or not, I'll be dealing with the infamous Terkel?"

"Don't know about *infamous*, but he's been brought into this because there's no way not to."

"Meaning?" Morrison hated that his tone sounded so cautious, but he'd heard a lot about Terkel. All of it was good, but it also made Terk seem way more powerful than an ordinary man. So maybe *too good*.

Levi laughed. "You'll see. You'll be meeting somebody else this morning too, one of Terkel's team."

"Why?" he asked bluntly.

"Your witness asked for one of Terk's men to be assigned to her case, as I was involved in setting up the meeting."

"Crap," Morrison muttered. "I really don't want to deal with anybody else."

"That's because you've been allowed to run the whole *lone ranger* thing for a long time," Levi pointed out. "You're an independent agent, aren't you?"

"Kind of, the relationship is complicated. I tried to retire, and they wouldn't let me, but I wouldn't go back to work under the same bosses. So *independent* is a good way to put it."

"Oh, I understand that totally," Levi replied, and indeed understanding filled his tone. "It's one of the reasons why we are where we are, independent and private. If you ever want to hook up with the group, let me know," he offered, "though I'm not so sure that you don't rightly belong with Terkel's group."

Morrison frowned at that, unsure what he was supposed to say and worried that a little more knowledge about him and his own abilities was out there than he cared to admit.

Levi laughed. "What? No comment?"

"Not sure what I'm supposed to say to that," he muttered.

"You don't have to say anything, but you should know that attempting to hide your abilities won't work with Terkel," Levi pointed out. "Just letting you know that upfront." And, with that, Levi rang off.

And his cell rang again almost immediately. He answered it cautiously, again not recognizing the number.

"We're not shitting on your parade," the caller greeted him, "but when an energy worker is in trouble, I tend to get brought in. So, yes, you'll be dealing with me too." And without giving him a chance to say anything in response, Terk ended the call.

Morrison pulled into the parking lot of the restaurant and sat there, contemplating these two phone calls. As phone calls went, this one from Terk was guaranteed to create unrest. Now it wasn't that Morrison didn't appreciate help or that he was anti-Terkel or anybody else for that matter, but Morrison didn't like people shitting on his plans, and that appeared to be exactly what was happening. For that, he could probably blame the woman waiting for him in the restaurant, assuming she would even show up.

When a vehicle pulled up nearby, and a woman got out and walked into the restaurant, he studied her, wondering if that was Sadie. A hard knock on his passenger side window had him jerking up and staring out at the newcomer. He rolled down the window.

The man bent closer, his face hard and his features like stone. "I'm Gage."

Morrison stared at him for a moment, sensing the power coming off him in waves. "You're part of Terkel's team."

Gage gave him a ghost of a smile. "I am," he declared. "Shall we go in?" He stepped back and waited as Morrison closed the windows, shut off the engine, stepped out, and locked up.

Morrison assessed the man in front of him, but no way to mistake the power, at least not if you were somebody who understood the feel of energy and who knew what it looked like.

Gage just waited while Morrison did his examination,

finally raising an eyebrow.

"Well?" Morrison asked.

Gage nodded. "I gather you're not happy at having your plans changed."

"Would you be?" He shot back a hard look at the newcomer's face.

Gage shrugged. "No, but you'll adjust. In a case like this, it's more about making sure we settle our differences and leave it be. You don't take it with you on the job."

"I don't even know you," Morrison muttered.

"No, and I don't know you either," Gage pointed out, "but I've been brought in on the case, so we'll have to work it out."

"All because of her word?" Morrison asked, with a nod toward the restaurant in front of them.

He nodded. "She called for Terkel, and when that happens? … Well, when it involves energy and energy workers, we're there." He smiled, looked over at Morrison, and added, "It's not as if you didn't already know that."

"Knowing something and actually dealing with it is a totally different story," he muttered. "You might deal with energy workers, but I don't."

"Yet you are one," Gage declared in such a calm, laid-back tone that it left Morrison staring at him in shock. Gage snorted. "I call it the way I see it, and, if you have any hopes of hiding it from other energy workers, that won't work."

"No, maybe not," he conceded, "but that doesn't mean I want the world to know."

"I get that, and I sure won't be saying anything to anybody," Gage shared, "but I do want to ensure that you and I are on the same page before we go in there."

"I don't know exactly what your skills are."

"I'm not sure in this day and age that any of us really know anymore," he admitted, "as ours are changing so much."

Curious, Morrison wanted to ask how and in what way, realizing that he'd never had a conversation with anybody who utilized energy.

Gage motioned to the restaurant. "She's waiting for us."

Morrison headed inside and walked up and sat down across from the woman he had watched get out of the vehicle just moments ago. He bent closer and, in a low tone, asked, "Sadie?"

She looked around nervously and nodded. "Yes," she whispered.

Gage sat down beside him so that the two of them faced her, yet it also blocked the rest of the restaurant from her view.

She shifted uneasily.

"Do you want me to move?" Morrison asked.

She shook her head. "No, not as long as you are part of Terkel's team, … it's all good."

"I'm not," he clarified, "but Gage is."

With relief, she looked over at Gage. "Does Terkel remember me?"

He nodded. "He does, although he doesn't have a whole lot of current information about you."

"No," she whispered. "It was a long time ago. I even met Celia a time or two."

Gage nodded. "And those memories, those connections," he noted in a soothing tone, "they're very important right now."

"Are they?" she asked, staring at him, fear evident in her gaze.

"Tell us how you survived the jewelry store robbery and how your brother avoided getting shot?"

She shook her head. "I wasn't there at the time. I came later to check on my brother, one of the guards there. He wasn't the guard who got shot that day."

Gage said, "Why don't you just tell us what this is all about?"

"The jewelry store robbers," she began, "I think, … I think my brother's one of them."

As opening gambits go, it was pretty stunning.

Morrison frowned. "Your brother, the security guard, was part of the jewel thieves crew?"

She shook her head. "No, turns out I was adopted, and the security guard brother I grew up with is not my blood brother."

Gage just stared at her, as she looked anywhere but at them. "You want to explain more about that?"

She snorted. "Not particularly, but I don't really have much choice. The thing is, my blood brother and I are not close, not at all. I don't know whether he's doing this on his own, or maybe he's being forced to do this. Of course I want to think he wouldn't do this, but I don't know that," she murmured.

"So how do you know he's involved if you're not close?"

She hesitated and then revealed in a low tone, "I read energy signatures."

"As in, you know the energy of somebody who has gone before you?"

She nodded. "I was visiting my adoptive brother, the guard in one of the jewelry stores that had been hit, just to make sure he was okay," she shared, shaking her head. "The robbery had been a while ago, one of the earlier ones, but I felt the energy, and, although faint, it was my brother's, my *blood* brother's."

"That's not damning. If you walked into that jewelry store right now, somebody else would recognize your energy," Gage stated. "Just because you saw his energy there doesn't mean he's connected."

"No, it doesn't," she admitted, with a shrug. "I know it's not enough, but I was suspicious. So I went to the next site of the jewelry heists and to the one after that."

Morrison stared at her, then sat back. "You're telling us his energy was at all three robbery locations?"

She nodded, then looked at him curiously. "Everywhere. … Wait a second. This conversation isn't freaking you out, but you don't work for Terkel?"

"I don't work for Terkel," Morrison repeated. "I guess you could call me a freelancer." She didn't seem to care what the label was, and he had to admit that most people didn't, … as long as they came to help. "So, why did you contact Terkel? Why not call the police?" Morrison asked her. She stared at him as if he was a fool, and Morrison already knew it was a foolish question. Still, he wanted to see if she understood where this investigation was heading and what was going on.

"I *could have* phoned the police," she admitted, with a sarcastic tone. "That would have been a great report. *Yes, officer, I recognized my brother's energy at each of these stores where there's been a robbery, yet I don't have any proof outside of that energy that he had anything to do with this.* Yeah, that would have gone over well."

"You still don't have a lick of proof," Morrison stated pointedly. "We can't just go on your word for it."

"No, of course not," she agreed. She looked over at

Gage, then back at Morrison again. "The thing is, I haven't seen my blood brother for a very long time." After hesitating for a moment, she then added, "When I say a long time, I mean a really long time."

"So then how do you know it's him?" Gage asked.

She stared at him steadily. "Because we're twins."

# CHAPTER 2

A S INFORMATION WENT, Sadie knew it was a bit of a shocker. She leaned forward and whispered softly, "Our birth parents passed away many years ago, when I was very young. We were placed in foster care, and, instead of adopting us out together, they split us up." She gave them all the details because she needed them to trust her.

"I was adopted by a family with whom I stayed basically all my life," she shared, "and I didn't even know I had a twin brother until a few months back. I always knew that somebody was out there or something was there, a pull of some kind. I didn't know about energy and such skills, not until I decided to go looking for answers, many years ago. That led me to Celia and one of her studies, which confirmed I had gifts. But it was my own mother, my adoptive mother, who finally told me that I had been separated from my twin at a very young age. I just learned this a few months ago, and I was furious initially when I heard I had a twin."

Gage and Morrison both remained quiet, and she went on to explain. "I tried to find him, I did, but it's hard to trace these children who are in the foster system and then get adopted. Plus … my gut instincts told me to stay away. And I know that sounds bad." They didn't say anything, just watched and waited until she continued.

"Anyway, I gave up trying to find him and to make contact. I didn't do anything more."

"So what prompted your adopted mother to tell you about your twin brother?" Morrison asked, frowning.

"My adoptive mother got very sick, and I nursed her for a couple years. Not long before she passed, she finally told me that I was adopted. That I had a twin brother. That they wanted both of us, to keep us together. Yet my brother was a handful. They couldn't handle him, so they made the hard decision"—she swallowed nervously—"to give him up. After hearing that, it took me a while to deal with all those secrets that she had kept from me. I guess I'm still dealing with that. I mean, I thought she was my mother. Why would I not?

"I thought the brother I grew up with was my brother. Why would I not? Keeping those secrets to unload on me, while losing her too, was just too much. I had so much anger for many reasons concerning just me. Yet I also felt anger that my twin brother was denied this home with me. I understand that he had issues, that clearly he needed help, and yet it was all more than my adoptive parents could give him, so they just gave him back … and kept me. I'm sure that fact has impacted my twin brother's life as well."

She sat here, collecting her thoughts for a moment. "Intellectually I understand that I'm not guilty of any of it, yet …"

Morrison nodded. "At the same time, you don't know any other way to feel … but guilty."

She looked at him and nodded. "Exactly, so, when I tell you it's his energy, believe me that I recognize that energy. I don't even know what he looks like, back then or now. I just know that we're fraternal twins, so he won't necessarily look exactly like me, but there should be some familiarity I would think, but who knows?" She shrugged. "According to my adoptive mother, when we were very young, just adopted by them, we looked quite different, were quite different, and so they fell in love with me, and they didn't fall in love with him."

"That had to really hurt him."

"I'm sure it did," she agreed. "I find myself wondering what he remembers and imagining a scenario that has me bundled up and loved, so I quickly forgot any unpleasantness, while he was lonely and rejected, with nothing else to think about but the unfairness of it all. Again, I'm not guilty of anything. I know that, yet it's almost like a survivor guilt thing, and it's eating me up."

"You feel guilty because you're the one who won the jackpot, while he got stuck in the system."

"I don't know what happened to him. For all I know he may have had a wonderful life somewhere else. Maybe it's the best thing that could have happened to him."

"Yet now that you know that he's involved in these jewelry heists, you're feeling even guiltier."

She winced. "How can I not?" she asked. "I mean, I don't know what went on in his life. I didn't know until a few months ago that I even had a twin brother, and that was enough to break my heart. While I didn't know anything about the situation back then, I've been struggling since learning about my twin brother, even more so since then finding his energy at all three crime scenes."

"These revelations are a shock."

"I've also been struggling with anger at my adoptive family because they chose to split us up, when, if we'd had the opportunity to grow up together, both of our lives would have been enriched," she murmured.

"Particularly since you were twins."

She nodded and stared down at the coffee cup in her hand. When a waitress came along and tried to fill it, she placed her hand over the top. "No thank you." As soon as the waitress left, she held her head up. "I can't stay." She looked over at the men. "I have a USB key for you," she murmured. "I know you'll probably need to talk to me again, but I do need to go to work," and, with that, she slid the key toward Morrison.

Oddly enough, she gave the key to him, not Gage. Morrison accepted it and asked curiously, "What is this?"

"That contains the only details I have on my twin brother. It's not very much, and it's probably of little-to-no value," she said in exasperation. "I feel like I'm betraying him all over again, but when I realized that people were dying and that he was involved? I couldn't … *not* …" she whispered, then looked around nervously. "I don't know if anybody else knows about me," she added, "but I have to admit to feeling a bit paranoid."

Immediately Gage leaned forward. "Any particular reason, or is something making you feel that way?"

She hesitated, then nodded. "It feels as if I've been followed a couple times."

"Any chance it's him?"

"Sure, there's a fair chance of that. I've told you already what I know," she stated, "how I wouldn't even recognize him if I saw him. However, if he had any curiosity or found out somehow that he himself was adopted, he might have gone looking for more information, and he has as much access as I do. Besides …"

"Besides what?" Morrison asked.

"What if he's like me? Another energy worker?"

"That is a possibility." Morrison glanced at Gage, as he

fingered the key in front of him. Then he faced Sadie. "I'll need your contact information too."

She whispered to him, quickly offering her address and her phone number.

He nodded but didn't say anything, and she sighed, already looking tired and worn out, even though it should be the start of her day.

"I'm a dental hygienist. I work fourteen hours a day, and then I'm off on Fridays. This is my last day before I'm done with this session. So, I very much want to have a few days to get over what I'm doing here. It took me a while to get up my nerve to even approach anyone, and even then I needed somebody like Terkel," she shared, looking over at Gage.

Gage was taking notes.

She studied his movements, realizing a certain practiced air to it. "And I know you need more information, but I don't have more to give. I don't have any proof that I'm being followed either."

"I wanted to ask about that," Gage added, "and I won't let you walk out on your own if you think that's a thing."

"I'm not sure. It's just a feeling. … You know how you can sense that something's wrong all around you? I've been having it quite a bit lately, but I don't have any concrete evidence to prove it. It could be …" She took a deep breath. "It could just be my own guilty conscience."

"That happens," Gage muttered, with a nod.

"Yeah, it does. I mean, I didn't even know about my twin brother until a few months ago, and here I am turning him in because I think he's involved in robberies."

"Remember that he or his crew are killing people too."

"Exactly," she muttered. "I can't in good conscience just do nothing."

SADIE GOT UP suddenly, then, looking around, she added, "I've got to go." And, with that, she raced outside, hoping to somehow get away from the memory of what she'd just done. Yet the thoughts of her twin brother involved in theft *and* murder were all too overwhelming. She had a long work shift starting soon, and she needed to get through it as best she could.

Having already had such a tough visit with the two men made for a hard start to her morning. As she walked out to where she'd had parked her vehicle, even now she had that same feeling—that sense of not only being watched, but this time almost a fatalistic memory of somehow being here before.

She got into her vehicle and started it up. When a hard knock came on her car window, she jumped in fright. Seeing it was Morrison, she rolled down the window. While she was relieved it was him, it still pissed her off. "What?"

"I'll follow you to work, so don't panic."

She frowned. "I'm fine."

"You might be fine, but, if you feel somebody out there is following you, is interested in you, or anything you're doing," he explained, "I want to check it out. We have to start somewhere."

"What about Gage?" she asked.

"He's contacting Terkel."

She let out her breath, feeling a rush of gratitude that maybe she wouldn't have to handle this alone. "Thank you," she whispered. She rolled up the window and waited for him to get into a vehicle behind her. Then she pulled out and headed to work.

# CHAPTER 3

T**HE BUSY NATURE** of Sadie's workday required her to focus, so, throughout the course of her day, at some point she had calmed down enough to put behind her the thoughts stirred up by the meeting that had started her morning. Punching out, she headed to her car. Reaching for the handle, she heard a man speak close by.

She froze, then turned to see Morrison walking toward her. She hated that all the fear came flooding back up to the surface, though it wasn't all fear. She smiled at him. "Hey, I wasn't expecting to see you tonight." She studied him cautiously. All she knew was that a part of the team working for Terkel was on the case, but this one wasn't with Terkel.

Although she felt the power behind him, she didn't know if he knew very much about it. If he'd been part of Terkel's team, that would have been a different story. Naturally she was left jumping to conclusions and trying to make an assessment that she couldn't really do without more information.

"I'll follow you home."

She stopped, puzzled, still assessing him. "Do you really think that's necessary?"

He nodded. "I do. I'm not sure what's going on or who might be involved, but it does feel as if it's an issue." He didn't add that he felt he had been followed recently too.

That wouldn't help her calm down any. Still, she hesitated, her jaw opening, only to slam closed again. He smiled. "I get it. You're not at all sure, not at all convinced. And I could be wrong. Still, I would rather be safe than sorry."

She nodded slowly. "Okay." Without another word she got into her vehicle, knowing she was leading him right to her home. She couldn't find any reason not to though, and she'd already given him the address. So, if he was any good at his job, he'd probably already cased it out and had checked for problems in the neighborhood.

It still felt weird, and she wasn't at all sure that she was doing the right thing. So she watched as he parked outside, while she pulled into her underground parking, turned off the engine, and got out. He strode toward her. She smiled. "See? Home, safe and sound."

"Good," he replied. "That's the way we intend to keep it."

She wasn't sure what to say about that. "Why is it I don't think I'll like something about your plans?"

"I don't know," he said, motioning her ahead of him.

Sadie frowned. It felt as if he stood on guard, almost as if he expected something to happen. That made her race to the elevator.

Then he stopped her and said, "We'll walk up the stairs."

She winced. "Fine, but I would just as soon not do that in these heels."

He studied them and smiled. "I never did understand why you gals wear heels."

"They look great getting to work and leaving," she replied. "However, at work, I wear comfortable shoes that I can stand in all day. The truth is, I really like to wear heels," she confessed.

"That's great," he noted. "They just don't make it easy to move quickly though."

"That hasn't been a priority in my life," she noted.

He didn't say anything but led the way to the stairs, and she realized there wouldn't be any getting out of it. At least she was only on the third floor. By the time she made it up to her apartment, she was surprised that her heels weren't bothering her as badly as she would have expected.

She unlocked her apartment and stepped inside, not sure what to do now. When he immediately came in behind her, she studied him closer. "Are you really thinking there's a problem?"

"Yes. I'm really thinking there's a problem," he declared, with a nod.

That just set her off. "If that's the case, I'll be very sorry I ever came to you."

"And yet, when another person is killed during a robbery, you'll feel even worse," he pointed out.

She sighed. "So, you're saying that it's my doing, yet I should be happy that I did it? This is getting convoluted."

"Something like that," he muttered. He quickly walked through her apartment, as if searching for somebody lying in wait. She hadn't even considered such a thing, until he came back out and announced, "It's all clear."

She sagged onto the couch and stared at him. "I wasn't even thinking that I was in danger, just being followed."

"Yet you don't know what's going on with your twin brother, and, if he has any idea who you are, it might very well change a lot of things in his life. Some of it may not necessarily be for the better. The other consideration is that, if you're using energy to sense him, maybe he is using energy to sense you too."

She winced. "That is something I've considered to some degree, as I mentioned back at the coffee shop. However, I don't have any answers for you because he's never made contact, and neither have I," she stated bluntly. "I don't expect a pleasant kind of contact, not when my brother is out there … for criminal reasons."

"Right, but, for all you know, he's grown up fully aware that you were out there in the background, having a nice life, while he didn't. You don't know anything about him."

"And yet you've had all day to work your end of this," she pointed out. "Have you found anything?"

"We're working with MI5 to get the adoption records unsealed," he replied. "There is the usual paperwork to go through."

"Not for MI5," she stated.

"I haven't had an update," he murmured. "Meanwhile, I've been scoping out the next jewelry stores that I think they might hit as well as keeping an eye on you."

She frowned at that. "I would much rather you worked on the jewelry store angle. Wouldn't that be time better spent?"

He nodded. "I get that, and it's all fine and dandy, until something goes wrong in your life," he shared. "Right now, you're the only lead we have, and we need to keep you safe."

At his phrasing, she winced. "Right, so it's not about whether I'm in danger or not, but whether I'll endanger your case."

He frowned at her and then shrugged. "Not the way I would have put it, but, if you want to say it that way, it's your prerogative."

She glared at him. "I would like to be thought of as more than a lead in a case," she muttered.

"Of course."

Then a boyish grin broke across his face, making him look charming. She quickly dampened down her feelings as she stared at him. "What are you smiling about now?"

"If I'm not smiling, you get upset, and, if I am smiling, you get upset," he said, chuckling. "Believe me that nobody thinks you're anything other than an asset at this point."

"Yet *an asset* feels very cold," she murmured. "I don't want to be an asset. I want to be treated as somebody who has made a very difficult decision and is committed to stand by it."

"And you are, and we appreciate that," he stated, studying her intently.

In that moment, it dawned on her that was at least *part* of the reason he was here. It wasn't just to keep her safe. "You just wanted to ensure I'm for real, didn't you?"

"I work with a lot of people," he murmured, then walked over to the living room curtain, pulled it back, and looked outside. "A lot of people say they can do things, say they can feel things, but, when it comes down to it, they can't."

"Ah, so you are questioning my gifts," she muttered. "I don't really know what all I can do or all of what I should do, but I can tell you one thing for certain. ... I can recognize my twin brother's energy."

He grimaced. "I'm sorry that you're caught up in this. You should be having a happy celebration, finding out that you have a brother, a twin brother, not feeling sadness that he's involved in this."

"I keep racking my brain," she shared, as she walked into the kitchen to put on a pot of coffee. "Just trying to see if there's any other explanation as to what he's doing and as to why he would be involved in something criminal like this. I keep looking for—"

"An excuse?"

"Yes, an excuse, if you want to put it like that. Anything that won't break my heart if he's involved because, if he's in the middle of it, then—" She just stopped, feeling the tears in the back of her throat.

He gently squeezed her shoulder sympathetically. "It's hard. I understand that. Whenever it's family, it's hard. It's even harder when it's family you haven't had a chance to connect with, and you've held off connecting with them for whatever reason. Right now, our priority is making sure that nobody else dies from his actions or from his involvement in this jewelry heist crew."

"It's hard to know if your brother has any abilities because, every place I've been, all the stores they've hit," he added cautiously, "there's been absolutely no sign of anything. I mean, obviously there are security cameras, and we get an idea of how many people, but the images are always distorted, so we can't even get any measurements of heights or descriptions or those usual things. We've been wondering if somebody is utilizing energy to help them pull off these robberies. So, when you came forward and thought this was potentially your brother, we're wondering if he is using his energy skills to hide their tracks."

She may have already had a simmering anger underneath, but that statement got to her. She sat down at the kitchen table. "I don't even know what I can do," she murmured, as she stared at him. "I see energy. That's all I know. I saw the energy as my adoptive mother passed away. I saw her soul slip free of her body and leave, but it was just this energetic form," she murmured. When his eyebrows shot up, she shook her head. "I don't know what I actually see," she admitted, her throat choked up again. "It's just been one of those things that happens in my life."

"Yet you know Terkel."

"I know *of* Terkel. There's a difference. I heard of him, when I was working with Celia, as part of her research into these abilities. She understands me better than I do," she explained. "I never worked with Terk directly."

"He says that he knows your energy though, so that would mean, in his world, that you work in the healing arts."

"Hardly. I'm a dental hygienist, so I don't think very many people would consider that among the healing arts."

"Yet you probably participated in a healing event with your adoptive mother."

She winced. "Right, so that would be considered the healing arts." She sighed. "What do you do when somebody passes, someone who spent their life raising you and giving you a good home? What if, in her passing, she shares a secret that devastates you? Up until that point in time, I did everything I could to make her passing as easy as possible, to make her whole illness as easy as possible," she shared, nodding. "I took six months off work to be her full-time caregiver, and only in the last couple days before her death did she tell me the truth."

Sadie shook her head. "I don't think she was even conscious after that," she murmured. "So, I never had a chance to ask her more questions or to rail at her for having done what she did." She stared at him. "Not having answers just eats away at you," she murmured. "It's ugly, and you want to know so much more, yet there won't be any more. It just is what it is."

"What about your adoptive father?"

"He had a heart attack and passed away a few months after Mom died." Then she stopped, frowned, and added, "I lost both of them in the last seven months." She sighed. "Time just got away in my world, and I didn't even know when I was coming and going anymore. You go from the death of one to the other, and you're numb to anything else. My adoptive mom was quite ill. So just trying to deal with her zapped all my energy, and then, when she was gone, she left me with this bombshell, and I'm still trying to sort it all out."

"She probably didn't dare tell you earlier, afraid that it would change the way you felt about her."

"Maybe." She stared at him. "I have to admit it would have, at least at first. Would I have hated her? No. She was still good to me, and looking after her all those months was something that I felt I owed her. Whether that was further bonding on her part, before she unloaded her secrets, I don't know, but I did feel strongly that I needed to do that. Now I'm at a loss. I went from having two loving parents to having two loving adoptive parents who rejected my twin brother because he was trouble. And I grew up thinking I already had a brother, but he was not my blood relative."

"So your twin brother, your blood brother, may have considered pulling the trigger on your adoptive brother. This alone shows you your twin's behavior in the here and now. Maybe your twin was already some bad seed even way back then, and your adoptive parents didn't feel they could cope with the added stress. Plus, as parents, I'm sure they felt very protective of their son and of you."

"That's pretty much what she told me. Yet, as the child who got to stay, I feel a certain amount of despair that my twin brother didn't get the same opportunities in life that I did. And now that I see what he potentially could be up to, it makes me wonder if that still would have happened if he had been raised with me."

MORRISON COULD SEE that Sadie was still grappling with the emotional bombshell her adoptive mother had shared from her deathbed, not to mention the accompanying grief and the sense of betrayal. He kept his tone calm and centered as he spoke. "Did she ever mention anything specific about what he did that upset her or what caused them to not want to keep him?"

She shook her head. "No, she was dying, and the last thing she told me was how I was adopted and how my twin brother wasn't. I tried to get her to talk to me further, but, once she had told me, that was all she wanted to do before dying. That just made it all the more frustrating." She dropped her head on her hands. "I mean, you hear about deathbed confessions and all," she admitted, "but I never expected to hear one myself."

"Of course not," he murmured, "and your adoptive father, he didn't say anything?"

She shook her head. "No, not to me. He avoided my questions, after Mom's death, saying he was still grieving her loss. Then he had a heart attack and never woke up in the hospital, so whether he would have chosen to share or not later, I will never know."

Morrison shrugged. "Sometimes people get away with not having to face up to what they've done, and maybe, in his case, he just believed that they'd done the right thing. People often do, without acknowledging what happened to the other person in the equation. And, if your twin brother was very difficult at a young age, I can't say that I blame them."

She got up, poured a cup of coffee, and muttered, "I understand, and I'm not sure that I could have adopted one without considering the fact that I couldn't handle the second one. I'm still grateful for the upbringing I had, and that just makes me feel even guiltier."

"Yet you're not guilty of anything," he reminded her.

"I know that. I do, but it doesn't really help either." He nodded and watched. She poured a second cup of coffee and handed it to him black, just as he'd had it at the restaurant.

He accepted it and added, "Until we find out more, I'll stay here."

She looked at him in surprise. "Oh, you don't need to do that," she countered immediately. "Even if it is my twin brother, how will he know that I'm involved? I don't think he even cares."

"Why, because he didn't follow up and find you?"

She stared at him, feeling that sense of betrayal again. "Yeah, I guess." She put down her coffee cup carefully. "I'm really messed up over this, aren't I?"

"It doesn't matter," Morrison replied. "We aren't look-ing for proof that any of this happened. We're just dealing with how to stop him and his crew now."

"Of course."

He grabbed his duffel bag and dropped it by the table. "Do you mind if I stay?"

"No, go for it."

"I'll ask about an update. Sometimes phone calls work, but we shuffle files back and forth quite easily too. They should have something on your twin brother at this point, I would think."

"I would like to know what they found out," she murmured. "My mother said his name was Don. Does he still go by Don? And what was his life like? Was it decent? I mean, I just hope he was treated okay and had a good childhood."

Morrison didn't say anything to that because he had seen kids with the best upbringings turn out to be absolute assholes, with no care for anybody else, and he had also seen kids with the absolute worst upbringings turn out to be wonderful people. So he wasn't sure that a happy childhood would make any difference.

Her twin brother was involved in something right now, whether he had chosen it or not. He was in trouble with the law in a big way, and, unless he had a hell of an explanation for why he was doing what he was doing, there wouldn't be an easy solution for him. Not in this lifetime.

Morrison turned on his laptop, then brought up his email to see if anything was there, and there was. He quickly brought it up and nodded. "They managed to get into the adoption records," he shared. "Your twin brother, Don, was adopted about six months after you were, and"—he kept reading silently, then involuntary winced. "His adoptive parents were killed in a car accident, and he was put back into the system."

At that, she sucked in a breath, and Morrison nodded. "That obviously would have an impact on him, even at a young age." He studied the file, knowing that the next part would upset her even more. "He was never adopted again, and he stayed in the foster care system, until he ran away at sixteen and again at seventeen. By the time he turned eighteen, they had no idea where he was. He'd been listed as a constant runaway in the system."

As she stared at him, he noted the flood of tears building

that she was desperate to control. Noticing a box of Kleenex nearby, he grabbed it and put it in front of her. "Best to just deal with it now," he suggested, as the tears began to slide down her cheeks. "You can only help him with so much. While I can see that his upbringing may have had a negative effect on him and how he's living his life now, I'll also tell you that an awful lot of good people are out there who had really crappy beginnings. They don't all end up murdering people in jewelry stores."

She swallowed and nodded. "I imagine drugs have a bad effect too."

"Possibly, but it doesn't say anything about drugs, substance abuse, or anything. He doesn't have a rap sheet," he added. "That does surprise me. Typically someone works up to major crimes like these, but he's what?" He checked the file to calculate his age. "He's twenty-eight?"

She nodded. "Yes, we're twenty-eight. Our birthdays are September 20."

He nodded. "So, we have enough years for him to form an opinion about life, society, what he'll do, good or bad, yet without a rap sheet. That doesn't make any sense with what we know at present. He hasn't done any jail time, which is a good thing, … but that is odd too." He shrugged. "He won't escape prison now, not if he's involved in this. Is there any chance that the energy you were sensing isn't his?"

"There's always a chance," she admitted, staring at him. "How would I know? Maybe ask Terkel that question."

He frowned but brought up his phone and sent Gage a message instead. When Gage phoned a few minutes later, Morrison put it on Speakerphone. "The reason I sent you that message is because Sadie was wondering if Terkel could double-check that question I had for her, but I thought you might know, so I'm checking with you first."

Gage sighed. "I can ask him, but I don't know if it's a thing either. It's energy at a distance, and I know that, in some circumstances, Terk has a way to check it out. I will relay your request."

"If it's my brother's energy, then should I just sadly accept that Don has gotten involved in something that's way over his head, and it is just a fact of life?" she cried out.

Gage hesitated and then replied, "Sadly that's not a bad analysis."

Morrison heard her tears showing up again, then spoke to Gage on the phone. "I just read the update with the history on Don."

"I did too. We don't have a last known address, but, once we got the name and details, we found that he did own a vehicle, and it was registered to a specific address, but we don't have him at that address any longer. It was about two years ago, and, since then, we have no record of his being at that address," Gage shared thoughtfully. "So, we're all still looking for him."

"Keep looking," Morrison stated. "Don's got to be somewhere."

"He's in hiding after these crimes, and, if he's been doing energy work for the heist crew, then maybe his abilities are more developed than Sadie's, and he ..." Gage let his voice trail off.

"Yes, we were thinking of that too. I keep coming back to the idea that somebody is hiding the energy and managing to scramble the electronics, so they aren't showing up clearly on the camera feeds. Maybe even jamming the alarm signals, if that's something Don can do too." He turned to look at Sadie.

Sadie shrugged. "I have no idea what he can or can't do, any more than I know what I can do myself."

"Got it. Gage, did you hear that?" Morrison asked.

"Yeah, I did. I also just got a confirmation from Terkel that the energy signature is a match for Don."

Hearing the wordless cry beside him, Morrison replied, "Okay, thanks for that. If you get any other updates, check back in. I'm at her place."

"You still feel she's not safe in that regard?" Gage asked curiously.

"It just feels wrong," he clarified. "I can't tell you how much or why, but something feels wrong, and I just know something's going on here. … I get that it's hardly the priority in this case, yet it seems as if it should be, you know?"

"Absolutely it is," Gage agreed. "I'm not telling you not to stick by her. I guess what I wanted to say is, watch your back." With that word of warning, he ended the call.

Morrison smiled down at the phone, enjoying a certain sense of freedom in working with people who understood energy. People who didn't double-cross you or question your choices. He could easily see doing this work with somebody like Gage again in the future.

"What are you smiling about now?" Sadie asked from across the table.

He looked up at her and realized that he had revealed his feelings. "It's just that I've never worked with anybody else who has done energy work before, and it's quite freeing in a way. Nobody questions my feelings, my thoughts, or my out-of-the-blue decisions, and there's this … sense of acceptance that I've never had before."

"I can see that." She nodded. "I just keep thinking that I

should be doing something more, especially if my brother is doing all this with his energy skills."

"And maybe you can. I mean, you can see his energy. And you saw your adoptive mother's soul leave her body."

"Yet I don't know that it was really her soul," she clarified. "I just saw what I would call energy."

"Not sure what anyone else would call it," he noted, with a gentle smile in her direction. He rubbed his stomach. "I will need food." She stared at him, not quite getting it until he asked, "I'll be your house guest, so are we ordering in, or do you have groceries?"

She blinked as if she suddenly understood where he was going with this and looked around. "Are you sure you need to stay here?"

"Yes, I'm sure," he stated. "I'm not willing to give on that point at all. I get that it wasn't part of the deal you were expecting, but the more I get involved in this, … the more I realize it's very necessary."

She shuddered, then nodded. "Fine, I have a house guest apparently."

"You do," he agreed, with a bright smile. "And thanks for not arguing about it."

She gave him a wry look. "Would it do any good?"

"No, it sure wouldn't." He chuckled. "However, it does make my life easier. Now, I do happen to cook," he shared, "but for that to work, you must have food here."

"Yeah, that's a bit of a problem," she muttered. "I've been so distracted in the last few months since all of this with my twin brother came up."

"Now's a good time to start eating regularly," he noted, "because one of the things about energy work is that you need to feed it. Plus, I enjoy being fed." He got up and walked to the kitchen, which was literally right beside him, and went to open the fridge, then looked at her. "May I?"

She snorted. "Odd that you should ask now."

"Hey, I did ask if you were okay with my staying, but considering that it'll save your life—"

At that moment, he realized the way he'd phrased it was one of the reasons he didn't do well in office settings or in teams. It was true as far as he was concerned, but he tended to just let the words come as they may, without giving people a chance to be prepared for it. Like Sadie. She just stared at him in shock, and he nodded because he had no choice. The cat was already out of bag. "Yes, I'm serious."

She swallowed hard, nodded several times, then got up and opened up the fridge. "You're right. We need to eat."

And, with that, the conversation completely detoured into food.

They both had things on their minds.

# CHAPTER 4

SADIE WOKE UP the next morning with a sense of wrongness filling her. Frowning, she slowly sat up, looked around her bedroom, then remembered the events of the night before. Not only had Morrison cooked dinner for her but the conversation had remained suspiciously free of any mentions of her twin brother, until a phone call came later that night. He'd looked at her pointedly and announced, "I need to take this in private."

She'd gone into her room and to bed. Now it was a new morning, a new dawn, and she had to face whether she asked him about the call or not. She got up, had a quick shower, and dressed in leggings and a T-shirt, then headed out to the kitchen, not surprised to find him there, already at work on his laptop.

He looked up and gave her a lazy smile. "Good morning."

"Good morning," she replied. "Did the phone call last night do any good?"

"No," he stated in a causal tone. "We were hoping that an address we had sourced would bear fruit, but it did not."

She didn't know if she should be happy or sad. "So, my twin's still at large then."

"He is, indeed. However, the address did lead us to another address, and we have a team there, watching to see if anybody shows up."

"Of course, and that'll be the thing now, right? We'll just hunt down my twin brother?"

He stared at her for a long moment before responding. "That's not quite the way I would put it, but, yes, given the fact that your twin brother is quite possibly involved in recent crimes. We're not pinning all our hopes on that of course," he added. "We're still looking to identify the rest of the crew members, therefore, trying to find more of his friends, his inner circle."

"Right, because he's not doing this alone."

"It looks to be four crew members."

Surprised, she frowned and stared at him. "Yes, I guess it takes that many, doesn't it?"

"Yep, so stand strong, and we'll get there."

"Maybe," she muttered. She walked to the kitchen and started pulling things out of the cupboard. Looking at him, she said, "I want pancakes. You want some?"

He beamed. "I would love pancakes."

With that, she got to work, as he took several calls behind her. Hearing some frustration in his tone, she shared, "You know you can go off and do your own thing, right?"

"Wouldn't that be nice," he noted, with a smirk, "but I'm the one who made your safety an issue. So nobody wants to let me do anything else."

"We could always drive around."

He looked up at her and asked, "What would that tell us?"

She stared at him and then shrugged. "I don't know."

"And yet that was the suggestion you just made," he pointed out, studying her intently. "Why?"

She frowned, turning back to the stove, pondering that

herself. "Maybe I would recognize his energy signature."

"Here's a question for you. If you were to recognize his energy, would you want to go see if he was there?"

"Remember that other energies were in the mix that I didn't recognize. However, it's often crossed my mind that maybe they must be local, right?"

"Sure, but this is also a large city."

"Yet all the jewelry heists were done in a fairly small geographic area."

"I know, and that's one of the reasons I've been keeping an eye on another nearby jewelry store, thinking that it would likely be targeted, maybe as their last and final job because it's a big store."

"Maybe," she muttered. "I mean, what's to stop them from doing this forever?"

"Nothing," he replied, "unless we stop them. Particularly if your twin has some way to knock out things, like the alarms and security cams."

"*Right.*" She groaned. "I just … I can't bear thinking about it. That gives them a huge edge, which is a terrifying thought."

"If you had been in the bank, I don't think you would be terribly happy to find yourself in the middle of a robbery. Other innocent people were around, including your adoptive brother."

"Not a bank, a jewelry store," she corrected.

"Sure, for the moment."

At that she spun around and stared at him. "Oh no," she murmured. "So, this could just be some practice run for them?"

"That's possible. Think about it. I mean, what's to stop them from going after banks, which is where the real money is? Both jewelry stores and banks have guards. So there is that extra element to consider when robbing one or the other. Right now, they either have a source for fencing the jewels or somebody in the private world is paying them to pull this off. But what happens when they decide they don't need to work for anybody else, and they just go out and get what they want? Granted, we don't know that this crew is funded by some collector or whatever. I'm just considering other avenues here."

"I understand. And the bank angle could be exactly what the crew hits next, or eventually. Particularly when banks offer a much bigger payday. And they get cash. No need for a fence or a pawn shop or whatever. God," she muttered, "I hadn't even considered that."

Morrison didn't say anything as he wanted her to gradually get there on her own. She quickly finished up the pancakes and brought them to the table, and, while they were eating, she contemplated her options.

"I have several days off now," she shared, "so why don't we drive around to some of the areas I was searching before? I found a couple places where I wondered if I was feeling Don's energy."

He looked at her in surprise.

She shrugged. "I was just trying to connect with him in some way, but maybe that connection brought in something else."

"You probably were connected with him," Morrison said, "but that doesn't mean he knows what you're doing, or that, if he finds out what you're doing, he'll be happy about it."

She stared at him, grimacing. "I did sense his energy somewhere else."

"In that case, as soon as we're done eating, we'll go for a drive," he stated. "Hopefully we'll turn up something before they hit another jewelry store and kill another person."

She winced at that. "It never even occurred to me that I could do something to actively help."

"You weren't quite ready to do anything before, so don't punish yourself for it."

"What if somebody dies in the meantime because I didn't?" she whispered.

"Realize that the gunmen are the ones responsible for killing people, not you. You can only do what you can do, but these gunmen are calling the shots. They are the ones making these decisions. We don't want anybody else hurt or killed, and we must stop this crew before they decide to start harvesting money willy-nilly wherever they want," he explained. "They do appear to have some energy-work techniques in play, something that's allowing them to get in and out much faster and cleaner than normal. That's not making any of us happy obviously, and putting a stop to that would give us an advantage."

"That makes sense."

"So, I don't know what all you can do with your particular gifts, but, if you can sense his energy in another location, maybe we can get a bead on it and can then have somebody else come help us with locating Don. Maybe Terkel has a team member who can help find Don."

SADIE DELIBERATELY SLOWED her actions to try and delay the inevitable, but Morrison finally got her into his vehicle. Slightly annoyed that he was in such a hurry, she asked why they were taking his vehicle.

Looking at her point-blank, he replied, "So you can't be traced back home."

She didn't say anything, but her face paled slightly, as she buckled in. He pulled out into traffic and headed down the street. Almost immediately she spoke up. "Turn left up here."

The instructions were as clear and crisp as day, and, when he soon pulled up near a pool hall, he stared at it, took out his phone, and snapped several photos of it. "Why this place?"

"It's where I recognized his energy. It's one of the things that got me started on this," she admitted. "I was down here, not at the pool hall itself, but at a fabric shop at the end of the block." She pointed, and, sure enough, he could see it. "Whenever I'm stressed, I tend to come here a lot," she murmured. "It's just a hobby of mine, and I wanted to look for supplies. I couldn't find parking, so I ended up walking past here, and I got hit with that same energy."

"Interesting," he noted. "It's definitely the kind of a place I could see Don hanging around."

"I didn't even realize what I was recognizing at the time," she murmured. "Of course now I don't know what I'm recognizing at all."

He squeezed her hand. "Let's go for a walk."

She got out of the vehicle and instinctively headed toward the clothing shop. He followed her inside, and she picked up a couple spools of thread that she apparently needed, which she quickly paid for. With a smile and a wave to the cashier, she headed back out, then looked at him and shared, "I didn't feel anything when we went by the first time, but a little coffee shop is just past it"—she pointed that way—"so we should head in that direction."

"Sure," he agreed, and they walked past the pool hall a second time. She shrugged and didn't say anything.

"Nothing, *huh?*"

She shook her head. "No, not right now."

And that would be the problem. However, if her twin had any affiliation with that pool hall, it needed to be staked out. He quickly texted his request for someone to be on the lookout there. "We'll keep an eye on this place. Now, where else?"

"How did you know there is another place?" she asked, frowning at him.

"Because you've been too quiet, as if you're contemplating whether you should tell me or not."

She winced. "The trouble is, it makes no sense."

"In what way?"

"It's a park," she replied, "like a playground for children. That's why I'm hesitant. It doesn't make any sense."

"Show me." She quickly gave him directions to the new location as they got back in his car. When he pulled up to the sidewalk at the address, it was, indeed, a children's park. What he found interesting was that Sadie stiffened almost immediately at the sight of the kids playing there. "So, do you want to explain that reaction?"

"I don't know how to explain it," she whispered.

"You need to though." He turned to face her.

She frowned, her gaze locked on a little boy and a young woman enjoying the park, laughing cheerfully. "Them," she said, with a headshake.

He turned to study them, then whistled. "You're telling me that your brother's energy is coming off them?"

"I'm telling you it's somehow connected. I don't know

how or why," she murmured, as if in a trance. But it was obvious from the transfixed expression on her face that this was not what she expected. From her family point of view, it changed things drastically. She turned to him, tears in her eyes. "What if he's just trying to provide for them?"

"By killing people?" he asked.

She flushed, then shook her head, sinking low in the passenger seat. "God, I don't even know what to think anymore."

"It's not an easy scenario for anybody, and we're not judging right now," he stated. "We just need to talk to him. That would make a huge difference."

"Maybe," she whispered, "but then again, there's a chance that maybe it won't make any difference at all."

"Don't judge him yourself, not until we have a chance to talk to him," Morrison stated. "If he is just trying to provide for them, I'm not sure she would be happy to find out Don's methodology."

"No, I wouldn't think so." Hesitating, she added, "It's not as if I can just walk up and talk to her either."

"Nope, you sure can't," he declared, "but we'll definitely do a rundown and see who she is and if there's any record on file of the father to that boy." With a text sent off, he tilted his head and looked at her patiently. "Now, a third place?"

She stared at him, frowning.

He lifted his eyebrows. "I can read energy too, and we need to be honest with each other," he said. "There's still something else bothering you."

She glared at him, then rolled her eyes, followed by a sigh. "When I was at the hospital with my dying mother, I felt something like ... I don't know."

He stared at her. That wasn't what he'd expected. "At

the hospital?" he repeated.

"Yeah, but I don't know what I was feeling, I just felt that same jolt of energy. It was the weirdest thing. I mean, I don't have any way to tell you more about it."

"Okay." He stared at the streets around them. "So, this happened during her passing?"

"Just afterward. I was sitting there, still stunned really, and it was almost like getting … an electric jolt," she explained. "I don't know what it was—or if it was even my twin brother—but considering that I went looking for him, based on that energy signal, I guess it makes sense that it was."

"So, hang on. Let me get this straight. Your adoptive mother tells you, just before she dies, about your twin brother. Then you have a sensation of him being around you soon afterward, and, based on that energy and what she shared, you started looking into it."

"Something like that," she conceded, with a nod. "God, when you say it that way, it sounds bizarre."

"I don't know about bizarre," he murmured, "but we do need to sort out whatever is going on here, just so we can get to the bottom of it."

She didn't say anything but nodded.

Morrison asked, "If we went to the hospital, could you go to any place in particular where you felt that jolt of energy?"

"The hallway," she replied. "I think he was just walking down the hallway. I don't even know that he knew my adoptive mother was in there. For all I know, he had a friend in the hospital and knew nothing about my situation there."

"Did this energy have …" He hesitated, then decided he better rip off the Band-Aid fast. "Did it have an emotion attached to it?"

"Fear," she said. "He was afraid."

"*Great,*" he muttered. "That could mean anything."

"Of course. It could suggest he was afraid for somebody in the hospital or even for himself. He may have been injured and was heading to the emergency room," she suggested. "I don't know what to say."

He studied her face, clearly seeing the honesty and the confusion, as well as the worry that nobody would believe her. He realized how hard it was to talk to people about energy who didn't understand it, particularly when you didn't understand it that well yourself. He'd closed off those doors a long time ago, so he didn't have to deal with this—the confusion and the inability to explain the unexplainable. Yet, here she was, trying to deal with the exact same thing.

He quickly texted someone. "Terk and his team can check the hospital records, see if any patient by the name of Don shows up. They can even check the hospital cams, try to find Don, a current photo of him. Obviously we'll be at an impasse for a little bit, while we sort out these three leads." He stared out the car window. "Let's go home. I've shared these three places with everybody, and we'll go from there."

She noted, "They're leaving."

Startled, he turned back to the park, and, sure enough, the woman and the little boy were exiting through the side gate.

Sadie suggested, "I think we should follow them."

"I'm already on that one," he confirmed, as he quickly turned on the engine and waited while the woman got the little boy settled in her car and headed out.

# CHAPTER 5

BACK AT THE apartment, Sadie couldn't settle. She paced and paced, and in between she put on more coffee, realizing she didn't need more, but drank it anyway and kept pacing.

Morrison looked at her time and time again. When it was too much for him, he had to intervene. "After she went grocery shopping, we handed her off. It was a strategic decision and a necessity. We did that so we weren't caught in the act," he explained, "and, no, I haven't heard any report yet from those who followed her."

She frowned. "Why did you come back here? We could have kept following her. She had no idea."

"Because of you," he added. "Your energy was getting pretty unsettled, almost as if it was surging all over the place. That isn't good if you don't want to be noticed."

"How am I supposed to be calm? There is a damn-good chance that was my nephew back there."

"Possibly, but how does that change anything right now?"

She slumped into the chair beside him and whispered, "It doesn't, yet in many ways it does."

"No," he corrected, "it doesn't. This is still a group of people killing others, and, on top of that, it's a group who is proving difficult to find. We have to figure out how to stop this crew."

"I know. I know," she cried out. "But now I worry about that little boy losing his father."

"For all you know, that little boy doesn't even know he has a father out there. For that matter, the father may not even know he has a son. Plus, we have no proof that Don fathered anyone at this time."

She took a slow, deep breath and nodded. "Good point," she muttered. "If my brother hasn't been very stable, maybe he was there with them and then gone."

"We have to give Don the benefit of the doubt, until more evidence comes in. Yet we can't let him slip through our fingers. Obviously the net is closing around him, and that's a good thing."

"And yet I'm part of the reason that net is closing." She stared at him, tears in her eyes. "And that makes me feel like shit."

"Would you like to go talk to the family of the security guard who just died?"

She flushed, looked down at her trembling hands, then whispered, "You know I don't."

He got up and crouched in front of her. "I'm not trying to be mean," he began. "This is not an easy scenario for you, and I get it. However, it's not easy for anybody else involved either. Four people are dead, and nobody in the gang of gunmen cared about them. They just shot them and went on their way."

She shuddered, but he didn't stop there.

"There was no need to kill people, but somebody in that group is trigger-happy. He's been a little too willing to let others die so he can get his stolen goods, and we can't let that continue. We don't yet know anything about this little boy in the park and have no confirmation that he's even related to you. So, let's wait until we get more information."

She stared at him and nodded slowly. "The problem with that is, what happens when they don't get back to us?"

"This is Terk's people. They *will* get back to us." He nodded. "I know that waiting is terrible, but jumping to conclusions—good or bad—isn't helpful either."

She didn't say anything but got up abruptly. "I'll go have a nap." She headed to her room and collapsed on the bed, pulling the blankets over her shoulders, as she tried to process everything going on. Just the thought that her brother had a child out there made her want to shake Don and to ask him what the hell he was doing that was more important than looking after that little boy? Yet she still had no idea if he even knew he had a son.

As she thought about the little boy she'd seen in the park, she recalled that he appeared happy and content, with a mother who really seemed to care. For that at least, she was grateful. She had no proof that he was her nephew, yet she also had a certain knowing within.

She didn't know if her brother knew of the child's existence. If he did, maybe he was okay with this estrangement. Maybe he was happy to let the mother go off and raise Don's child all alone, even though he himself had been adopted and then returned, left to the cold and lonely realities of the foster care system.

She couldn't even imagine what Don had gone through because, although some counseling had probably been available, how often did that ever help? Particularly at that age? He had lost his adoptive family and had been put back into the system, instead of going to the extended family of his biological parents. Why didn't someone else take him? Could it be they couldn't handle him, or maybe they just didn't want him?

Without children of her own, she couldn't even imagine the thought process that went into that or how hard it would be to make that decision. It couldn't be easy, and all she could do was hope that this would be over soon and that she would get to meet her twin brother, assuming he didn't wind up dead in a shootout. She had no doubt that, since people were dying during these crimes, the police would shoot first and would ask questions later. They had to get this stopped, and, one way or another, these gunmen would go down. She would simply have to make peace with the fact that she had a hand in it. And that, if something didn't break to help them save Don first, that little boy maybe could lose his father.

It tore at her, inside and out, to even think that her brother was this far gone. Yet she didn't have a hand in his current activities; she couldn't have. The crimes weren't her fault, but still, the grief ate at her. When a knock came on her bedroom door, she called out to Morrison, "Come in."

He opened the door, checked on her, and smiled. "Hey," he greeted her in a soothing tone. That voice of his was so serene and gentle that it brought tears to her eyes. She'd never met anybody so empathetic, while he helped to tear apart her world.

"So, I know the news is not always what we want it to be," he began, "but I can tell you that your brother did not father the boy we saw earlier."

She frowned. "But I felt Don's energy around them."

"And there could be many simple reasons for that. Maybe Don took an Uber, and then this mother and her son took the same Uber," he suggested. "Yet the father of that boy listed on the birth certificate was not Don. We have people going to talk to her right now, but the neighbors have already been contacted and so far it looks as if there's been no sign of your twin brother being there."

"So she probably doesn't even know Don," she muttered, sitting up against her headboard to stare at him.

"True, but it's a lead we need to follow. Don't get too excited. These are hard truths and not ones that you may want to hear," he acknowledged, raising his hands in peace. "You have a glorified vision of family that I'm sure doesn't match Don's experience at all. Regardless, now is not a good time for fanciful dreams but to face reality."

"I just feel so helpless doing nothing," she muttered, staring at him. "I need to do … something."

"What is it you want to do?" he asked, sitting down on the side of the bed.

She frowned at him. "I don't know. Even if we just drove around, hoping to get that energy jolt, I would feel as if I was doing something at least."

"We can go driving. I'm totally okay with that. I like driving." He shrugged and added, "We can check all the normal places that Don hangs out at—or just drive aimlessly if you want."

"As long as we could pick up anything on that, it would be some help, right?"

"Absolutely it would help," he stated, nodding in agreement. "We might find the juncture where Don's and Penny's paths crossed. However, we really need to locate your brother."

"Right," she murmured. "So, keeping that in mind, I want to go for a drive, just drive around, find a few places, do a few things. That would be okay, right?" She hopped off the bed, forcing him to stand.

He eyed her. "Do you always get this … unsettled?"

She nodded. "I do. It's like … it's as if somebody walked over my grave."

His eyebrows shot up at that. "Interesting choice of words and not exactly a phrase I would use in this instance."

"No, maybe not," she murmured, "but it feels right."

"That's usually somebody stalking, somebody reaching out to talk to you." He hesitated and then asked, "Have you at any point in time had anybody reach out to you, energy-wise?"

She frowned at him. "You mean, like my twin brother?"

"Yes, Don or maybe other strangers."

"No," she replied, "at least none that I recognized. I've really only been doing this since I found out about my twin brother."

"Maybe you should sit down and try it tonight before you go to bed. Just open up and see if anybody out there is trying to contact you. You might be surprised."

Later that night, rather than taking Morrison at his word—and certainly not ready to open up her senses to anybody who might be wanting to contact her—she turned instead to social media, now that she had a name for the girlfriend. *Penny*, and her son's name was Anderson. These two crossed paths with her twin brother. She knew it was a long shot, but it was the only shot she had right now. So she looked for information on the family, and when she came across it, she was delighted. She walked out to the living room to find Morrison still working.

"I just found Penny on social media."

He looked up at her with interest. "Anything on it?"

"Lots of playdates and stuff," she murmured. "Yet nothing about her partner. I've gone back as far as I can, but, since I'm not friends with her, I can't see a whole lot." She sat down and showed him the links.

Morrison nodded. "We can get more than this, but hunting social media is always a good way to see what people are up to. It might lead us to a connection for Don."

"Right. People post the darndest things." She shrugged. "I mean, when you think about it, if you don't have someone out there trying to do you harm, why not?" she murmured. "At least that's how most people feel about it."

He studied her face for a moment. "Do you post?"

"I have in the past, but not recently, not since my mother passed away," she clarified. "I didn't have anything happy to share. I usually told people what was going on in my world, so, other than that, nobody really expected me to post." He didn't say anything, and she immediately took that to mean something was wrong. "So, because I haven't been posting, that's wrong?" she asked, staring at him.

"No, not at all. Not wrong. It's interesting what you consider to be totally okay to post on social media."

"I've never really been big on it. I would rather meet friends in real life," she pointed out. "And spending as much time as I did nursing my mother, it wasn't something I kept up with."

"Boyfriends?"

She nodded. "When I had a serious relationship, I certainly posted about it, but I had more girlfriends back then too. Everybody was doing it. I just didn't find the need to keep it up. What about you?" she suddenly asked him.

"I don't post at all," he murmured. "Social media's got some serious issues, and, being in the line of work I'm in, it's a *hell no* for me. I'm very private that way, and I don't particularly want anybody knowing what I'm doing."

That didn't surprise her at all, and neither did the fact

that he didn't use social media. Several of her friends had gotten away from it over the years, but that also meant losing track of people if you didn't make the effort to keep in touch. It was far too easy to lose them along the way. "I think it's just become an easy way to let people know you're still on the planet," she added.

At her phrase, he smiled. "I agree with you on that, but it lets everybody else know that you're on the planet too," he stated. "Not something I'm too keen on sharing."

She burst out laughing. "I guess in your business that's not exactly a plus, is it?"

"No, it sure isn't," he agreed, with a grin. He clicked on a few of the social media screens, looking at the Friends list. "I was hoping your brother might be here."

"I looked," she confirmed, "but I couldn't see him."

"And that also tells us that he wasn't in her usual group, just somehow they crossed paths."

"Lots of guys don't want their personal life on social media," she noted. "So, it's not as if you're very different."

"No, but still, lots of them do share online," Morrison pointed out. "A lot of them don't care. In my line of work, we always track people through social media." He shrugged. "I haven't heard from anybody about this, but I'm pretty sure people have been checking out her links and all the rest. So nothing pertinent to Don was found, or I would have been notified."

"*Right,*" she muttered, with a growing awareness that just because she was checking social media didn't mean a dozen other people weren't as well. "I never really thought about it. Guess it was dumb of me to think that maybe it was something nobody else had thought of.'

"I would certainly hope so. It's an amazing part of our

world, when you think about it." Then he went back to the paperwork in front of him. As she sat here pondering what to do next, he suggested, "Feel free to go to sleep if you're tired."

"And if I'm not?"

He looked over at her and added, "Turn on the TV or do whatever you would normally do right now." He wasn't even looking at her now, focused on whatever he was working on. "Don't let my being here stop you from your normal routine."

She snorted. "How can it *not* stop me? It's not as if I can just ignore your presence."

"Yeah, … I guess that's a valid point. I wasn't really expecting you to feel obliged to stay up or to change your routine because of me. That's not what I would want."

"No, maybe not," she said, "but I still can't just ignore that you're here or that my twin brother is in trouble. Maybe I have potentially more family out there I don't even know about."

"Potentially family who may not want to know about you," he reminded her.

She winced. "Thanks for putting it in perspective."

"Look. I'm not trying to be difficult," he added, "but, until we have more facts, you need to consider all options, not just the *happily ever after* ones."

"You're right. I get it," she grumbled, throwing up her hands. "Maybe I'll grab a book and just go to bed."

"That sounds like a good idea," he agreed. "Something to help calm you down and to take you out of this funk for a bit."

"If that's even possible," she muttered and then gave a headshake. "Sorry, there I go again."

He laughed. "It's all right. You're allowed to be con-fused, disoriented, upset. I mean, all this is new to you, and, even when it's not, when it's personal, it's still new to you because you don't have any experience with it on that level," he revealed, totally understanding. "I know how hard it can be. You're not doing anything that the rest of us wouldn't do in a similar situation."

She wasn't sure how to take that but knew he was trying to help. She nodded. "I'll go have a bath and try to relax. If anything happens, you'll let me know, won't you?"

"I will," he stated, "and you're not expecting anybody, right?"

"No, not expecting anybody, and it would surprise me if anybody showed up," she shared. "I live a very quiet life."

"Maybe Don does too," Morrison noted. "Twins often share the same traits, even when raised separately. At least that's what some studies show."

Sadie frowned at that, considering it.

"Since when have you led this quiet life?" Morrison asked, turning to face her. "Or is it mostly because of being a caretaker for your mom?"

"Mostly, at least for the last six months of her life any-way. When you spend six months in the darkness like that, you lose an awful lot of friends because they've moved on."

"Not if they're real friends," he replied. "They'll proba-bly be there when you get back to life."

"Maybe, and maybe I just don't want the same things anymore. I guess this whole thing has shifted the way I look at life."

"That happens, and it's not a bad thing," he noted. "If you think about it, an awful lot of change can happen, and there's no reason that some of it can't be a good change."

Pondering that, she headed to her bedroom, decided to forgo a bath as it just felt wrong while he was here. Instead she grabbed a book and tried to read a little bit. At least until she could fall asleep.

When she heard his phone beep and his voice rage, she immediately bolted out of bed and raced to the doorway to try and listen in. "I'll tell her," he muttered in an undertone. "Yeah, no, maybe I should wait for morning."

"Screw that," she muttered, then stepped out into the kitchen, where he was on the phone.

He looked up, saw her there, and shrugged. "She's here now," he said to whoever was on the phone with him. "I'll get off here and call you back in a minute."

As soon as he ended the call, she stated, "Just to be clear, don't *ever* wait until morning to tell me something."

He smiled, then nodded. "It's not super important. It's … more or less just another piece of the puzzle."

"At this moment, any pieces of the puzzle are super important," she declared. "So, what did you guys find?"

"They found another woman who's connected with your brother, at least per social media. Apparently they crossed paths at the pool hall, although she claims to have not seen him in the last few weeks. Don was inconsistent about showing up."

"Oh, that's interesting," she murmured. "So, did this woman know Penny?"

"No. She didn't know about Penny or her son."

Sadie nodded. It's what she expected, yet it was disappointing. She wanted her brother to be this great family man, who would have learned from all the crap that he'd been through, but just because she wanted it to be true didn't make it so. "Could this new woman tell you anything about where Don could be?"

"She gave us a couple more names of guys he hung out with, but they were an ugly crowd that she didn't want anything to do with; and that's partly why she didn't get too friendly with Don. She didn't really have anything else to add. Don's not working, and she told our guys that was another problem with him. Don talked about plans but never really acted on them. She didn't know anything about his friends other than a couple nicknames," Morrison shared, "and we're trying to get a handle on those. She did confirm that he hung around that pool hall a lot." Morrison didn't add that drugs were known to exchange hands in that location as well.

Sadie stared at him and then nodded slowly. "That confirms that location then," she muttered.

"It also means that we got the information, and not just from you," he reminded her.

"And that matters?" she asked.

"It might to you, in the sense that, if Don blames anybody. he can no longer blame only you for that."

"I suppose," she muttered, staring around the kitchen. "That does make a logical kind of sense. It's just hard finding out that the blood brother you had high hopes for is turning out to be a louse."

"Don't know if he's a louse or just somebody who took a wrong turn in life. Or, in his case, was not given many opportunities to make a right turn at any point," Morrison added. "I'm not blaming him for anything at this point, not until we have the evidence to do otherwise. Again, we still have to talk to him."

"Right," she murmured, "and to not jump to any conclusions."

He nodded. "I know it's hard because you want answers, and we want answers too. But more than that we also need to know where he is and get this thing stopped, before anybody else gets hurt."

MORRISON WATCHED SADIE head back to bed again, knowing how hard this must be, yet not very many people would even consider her feelings in this issue. Her twin brother, if he was the gunman involved, had murdered several people, or at least appeared to be involved in heists that ended up with several people dead. Morrison had to keep reminding himself that, although the guy looked to be right in the middle of it, Morrison still had no confirmation of that yet.

That was a turning point from which there would be no going back. Sadie could always try for a relationship while Don was in prison, but, if Don was an angry young man, there was a good chance that he would rebuff any attempt she made. Morrison was sorry for that, but that couldn't stop or even change his investigation in any way.

Morrison eventually fell asleep on the couch, not hearing anything from Sadie's bedroom. He was a light sleeper and would know when she got up next. However, he didn't sleep too long at a time and expected to be the first one up regardless.

THE NEXT MORNING Morrison brewed a pot of coffee, anticipating Sadie would be up soon. Yet she seemed to be sleeping today—or maybe had a hard time falling asleep. When Sadie finally got up, she immediately headed to the kitchen. She thanked him for making the coffee and had a cup or two. It wasn't long before she started to fidget.

After she wiped off the counter for the third time, Morrison asked, "Do you want to go for a drive now? Maybe back to the pool hall? It's early, but who knows what we might see."

She immediately nodded. "I don't know why, but sure."

"I want to see if you can pick up any more of Don's energy."

"Of course you do," she grumbled in a wry tone. "I want to catch sight of my brother, and you're here trying to capture him."

"My agenda could hopefully result in giving you some time with him."

She stared at him and nodded. "I can't ever forget the fact that he's involved in something so ugly, can I?"

"It would be better if you don't forget it," he stated. "An awful lot of people out there want to stop Don and his crew right now, before anyone else gets hurt."

"Oh, I hear you," she murmured. She looked down at her watch. "It is early. Do you think it's too early for the pool hall?"

"Maybe," he replied, as he studied his watch, contemplating it. Just then his cell went off. He answered it to find Terkel on the other end. "Terkel, what's up?"

"They hit another jewelry store early this morning. The staff was just getting ready to open." Terk shared the location data—not the big jewelry store Morrison expected the crew to hit, but bad anyway.

"Ah, crap." Morrison sat back, sending a look to Sadie.

"Did they shoot anybody?"

"They did, but he's still alive."

"Thank heavens for that," he muttered.

"We don't know that he'll make it," Terk clarified, his tone hard. "Now, I don't know that you'll be allowed in, but I want you to take her down there and see if she picks up on her twin brother's energy."

"Yeah, I'll take her to the crime scene, and then I guess we'll go with the flow. We won't be allowed in the hospital, will we?"

"No, absolutely not," Terkel noted cheerfully. "You probably don't need to be there anyway. It'll be a hot case. Given the nature of the crime, the cops will be all over the victim."

"But if he's not dead, the gunmen may go back and try to finish the job. Particularly if the guard saw something, knew something, or was involved in something. Otherwise there would be no need for the crew to finish the job."

After a moment of silence on the other end, Terkel added, "Agreed, and I think that's highly probable in this case. I'll talk to the police about added security."

"I don't have a good feeling about this at all."

"No, neither do I." With that, Terkel rang off.

Morrison sat here, staring at her.

She flushed. "Somebody else is dead, right?"

"Not dead," he corrected. "Another store was hit this morning, just as they were getting ready to open," he explained. "Somebody was shot, but he's still alive."

"That's why you were asking about the hospital?" He just shrugged. "I don't have any reason to go in and see him either," she muttered in a contemplative tone. "I don't know any of these people, but I would like to go to the scene if I could."

"Terkel's arranging it right now," Morrison stated. "It'll be a madhouse because forensics is still on the scene, so we might not be able to get you in."

She nodded. "I should be able to get close enough though."

"Let's go."

And, with that, they walked down to his car. As she got in, he saw the disquiet on her face. "I'm sorry. Just when we think that maybe we can find an answer that's workable, something else goes wrong."

"In this case there are no workable answers," she muttered. "I mean, just because this man's not dead doesn't mean that the last one didn't die, and that'll be held against my brother and the other members of his crew."

"It absolutely will," Morrison confirmed. "No way these murders will be forgotten when it comes to jail time. Sentencing will be extra hard. These people at the store were just doing their jobs, and they were targeted because of it."

She sucked in her breath and nodded. "It's not a good time to work in a jewelry store."

He winced at that. "I wonder if that has anything to do with it."

"What do you mean?"

"Just … why jewelry stores? Like I mentioned earlier, banks would be easier."

"Except banks have their safes," she noted, "the vaults. Not to mention maybe armed guards, extra security and all."

He nodded. "I do keep wondering why not hit banks, but vaults do change the odds. Yet I still think this crew might be working on their targets from an energy aspect, messing with cameras and other security elements, possibly with the thought that they might switch it up at some point."

She didn't say anything more. As they neared the latest crime scene, she got more and more tense. He studied her when he pulled up outside the chaos. "Okay, so I understand that this is unnerving for you, but you're getting … I don't even know how to say it, but you've been tensing up constantly the closer we got."

She nodded. "Because I can feel my twin brother's energy," she stated, "and the red wave of anger enveloping him."

"Did you feel the same anger last time?"

She shook her head. "No, I didn't."

He pondered that. "Any idea why this time?"

She stared at him. "I don't understand anything about last time, so I don't know why this time would be any different, except the energy is fresher today. None of this makes any sense."

Morrison frowned. The fact that these guys were moving as quickly as they were meant that either they had a game plan, or were trying to execute something as fast as possible so they could get out of town. Which made a lot of sense to Morrison. On the other hand, Sadie was oblivious to how this all worked. Morrison couldn't take the chance of Sadie being seen constantly at the crime scenes. At some point in time, everybody's luck ran out, whether they were using energy or not.

The fact that this criminal crew could be using energy was something that still floored Morrison, and yet why not? He used energy, Terkel did, as well as the rest of his team. The fact that Morrison hadn't come across criminals who were energy workers before this caper didn't mean it wouldn't happen again. That it hadn't happened before this actually came as a surprise.

Unnerved, Sadie got out of the vehicle. As she approached the jewelry store, two police officers stopped her, Morrison immediately stepped up and explained who he was and who had sent him. One of the cops made a phone call, and somebody from the far side came over to talk to him.

As soon as he confirmed and identified Morrison, "Fine, but you can't go into the building itself."

At that, she nodded. "That's fine. I don't need to." She looked over at Morrison and nodded. "It's definitely him," she whispered.

"Can you get anything else?" he asked in a low voice as they got a little closer to the building but stayed well out of the way.

She sighed. "I'm not really getting anything else."

"Okay, and do you have anything that's helpful?"

"All I can tell you is that he's really angry. Something went wrong this time, and I don't know what happened, but, to him, it matters a lot."

"What's different this time is the fact that the guard is not dead."

She winced. "How does that make any sense about why he would be so angry?" she muttered.

"Because potentially, in his world, this needs to be all encompassing, with no witnesses," he suggested. "So, you have to keep that in mind."

"Is he that far gone?" she asked in a soft voice. "Definitely not the personality I was hoping for."

"Of course not, and understandably you've romanticized the idea of having a twin brother, so you have a soft spot for Don. It wouldn't have occurred to you that he might be a hardened criminal who wants absolutely nothing to do with anything, and whether it's his fault that he ended up this way or not is beside the point because this is where he's at."

Morrison wished he could make it sound better than that, but it was a difficult situation for both of them. He was interested in stopping Don and his crew, determined, in fact, since they were seemingly on this rampage to hurt as many people as they could. This couldn't continue, and Sadie needed to know that. She did in a way, but she needed to understand it all. She did in a sense, but was still trying to find the harmless little twin inside this grown man who was busy killing people for money.

When Morrison's phone rang again, he noted another call from Terk. "We're at the crime scene. Don's energy is here."

Terk added, "I have more *good news*. Put me on Speaker, so Sadie hears this."

Morrison grimaced but did as Terk instructed.

Terk began, "Sadie, you won't want to hear this, but you need to regardless. We've seen Penny show up on the street cams near each robbery. She seems to be the gunmen's hired driver. What a small world we live in that Penny is driving the getaway car for Don. That explains why his energy was found around her. She has just been named one of the four-member team for these heists and will be under constant surveillance from now on." Then Terk disconnected.

Sadie took several deep breaths, then whispered, "I guess I just have to say goodbye."

"To what?" he asked.

"To that fantasy of having a nephew, to getting to know my twin brother."

"I'm sorry you lost a potential nephew, but unfortunately Don's still there, and it appears that he's buried under a whole lot of anger."

"And that's the thing," she noted. "I hadn't really noticed the fury in his energy before, but this time it's very dominant. It's almost raging."

"And it would be good if we understood why," he stated, "but the only obvious thing that's different this time is that the guard isn't dead, not yet. Maybe your adoptive brother being *the guard who got away* changed the mind-set of the crew, where they got more bloodthirsty."

She nodded, looked up at him, and whispered, "Please, can we leave now?"

Immediately he moved them back to the vehicle, then helped her inside and quickly drove away.

# CHAPTER 6

As Morrison drove through town, Sadie gasped out loud, grabbing her arm.

"What's the matter?" Pulling over to the side of the street, he frowned at her.

She stared at him in shock, then shook her head. "I don't know. Something slammed into my shoulder."

He hesitated. "I hate to ask, but is there any chance it's your twin?"

She frowned. "I don't know. I don't know why it would be." Then she looked around, bewildered. "But, yes, there is a chance that it could be, although I've never had a reaction that was so strong and so painful like that. It feels almost real."

"You did say he was so angry," he reminded her.

"He is, but why is he angry at me?" At that Morrison shrugged, and she took a deep breath. "This feels very much directed at me."

"That changes everything. If it's directed at you, then he knows about you, and he's very angry and—"

"In pain, … lots and lots of it," she whispered, without even realizing that she was now engulfed in all his pain too. Almost instantly a new wave hit her, and then another wave hit even harder. She sat here, gasping for breath in the vehicle.

He placed a hand atop her arm. "Can you push it back?"

She turned to him, knowing the pain was evident in her gaze, but struggling, desperate to do anything that would help, as she whispered, "Shouldn't I try to follow it instead?"

He stared at her and gave a clipped nod. "If you can, yes. That's exactly what we need."

She nodded and pointed in the direction of the corner up ahead. "Up there, take a right. He's going right through that building."

"Is he in the building?"

"No," she muttered, gasping as another wave hit her.

"Is his anger directed at you?"

"I think it's directed at the world around me. He's so angry about something, incredibly angry, and I don't know why." Morrison started up the vehicle. Following her instructions, he went around the corner and then another, now headed down a stretch of road that seemed to go on forever. Meanwhile, he kept looking at her as he drove, careful to keep an eye on the road as well.

She shrugged. "Keep going. Keep going." He kept at it, and they finally ended up at another set of apartment buildings, when she cried out, "Stop." Then the pain eased. She straightened up, looked around, and frowned. "It's gone."

"What's gone?"

"The pain."

He studied their surroundings. "Any chance he recognized that you were here?"

She gave a harsh laugh. "I don't know very much about this stuff, so I don't know what's possible and what's not. It could just be that he's either fallen asleep or has some other way to ease his fury, and it just happened to take effect right now."

He nodded, got out of the car, and looked around. "Just the one large building is here."

"Whatever it was, it came from there," she whispered.

He got back in the vehicle and phoned Terkel, then quickly explained what had happened.

"Good," Terkel replied, "something for us to check out. Give me the address, and we'll start running it down."

"That'll take a long time, and it looks as if a lot of people live here," Morrison added. "It's got to be twenty stories high." But he gave him the address anyway.

Terk snorted. "Won't take us that long. A lot of people are here in the compound, helping out on this investigation between other jobs. Plus, we have a finder of our own, Langdon, who is on it too. He helped us a lot with Penny. Still, doesn't hurt to have boots on the ground. So can you guys stay there and see if Don comes alive again?"

"We can certainly sit here and wait a bit," Morrison replied, wincing at Terk's phrase and looking over at Sadie questioningly.

She nodded. "Yes, we should wait. I don't know what's going on, but Don's here, or at least he was." She frowned. "It's possible he left too, when the pain left."

Morrison relayed that information, then realized it was pointless and put it on Speakerphone, moving the phone a bit closer to her. "Terk, you're on Speaker now, so I'm hoping we can get more answers."

Terkel, his voice calm and reassuring, turned his attention to Sadie. "When the energy hit you," he began, "can you describe what it felt like?"

"A punch," she replied immediately. "Like somebody attacking the same spot over and over again," she described. "Even now my arm is killing me." She kept massaging it, then looked at it and winced. "I don't know if this is even possible, but I think I might have a hell of a bruise tomorrow."

"Chances are you will," Terkel confirmed. "This often manifests in very strong physical forms."

"No kidding. … It hurts like hell."

"I know," he said, his tone soothing, "feels like a charleyhorse kind of pain. On the other hand, this is excellent work, and we now have another location to go on."

"And yet it's not that helpful because I can't see or feel Don now. I don't know where he is, and this is a huge building. Hundreds and hundreds of people could be in there," she noted.

"That doesn't matter, but now we also know that he's connected to somebody there," Terk pointed out. "That means everybody gets a heavy perusal. I've got every available person here on it, and I'll contact the government and MI5 and get them on it too. I don't want to start evacuating the building until we know for sure that Don's in there. It is a possibility that the reason your pain stopped *was* because he left the building. Maybe something about that location makes him angry. Maybe he works with somebody in there."

"Oh." She frowned at Morrison. "It didn't occur to me that maybe he left. I didn't feel the energy move."

"Maybe there's something to that too," Morrison said. "Another reason to not evacuate an entire building just because of it."

"No, of course not," she agreed. "I will feel terrible if I turned out to be wrong."

"You're not wrong," Terk confirmed, "but interpreting the messages is the challenge." Terk then terminated the call.

Sadie frowned and shook her head, not knowing what

else to say.

Morrison asked her, "Are you okay?"

"Yeah. … I mean, my arm still hurts, but it's good. How is that even real? I had no idea it could manifest in a real form like this."

He shrugged. "I don't understand how a lot of this stuff works," he admitted, "but I think the trick is not necessarily to understand but just to accept that it works and go with it. Too often we get bogged down needing to know exactly how something works, but it's just a tool. So, if you learn how to make good use of the tool, it doesn't really matter how it works. Think about it. You don't look at a light switch and try to figure out how or why it works. You know it supplies electricity, so you just flip the switch."

"That simple, *huh*?"

"Yes, sometimes it really is. That's exactly what this is. Energy is a tool, and when we have the ability to use it, you just do. It's another tool in our toolbox, and you're lucky enough that you can wield it."

"But I'm not wielding it," she wailed. "I'm being wielded on."

At that, he stopped and frowned at her. "That is a very interesting statement."

She blinked at him several times. "But is it a good one?"

He gave her a small smile. "Maybe not from your point of view, but I definitely need to let Terkel know." He quickly texted him.

"Don't you want to call him?"

"I could, but the door is closed."

She stared at him. "What? Hey, you're the one who does energy work. I'm the newbie."

He nodded. "When I think about texting or phoning

Terk, I get an almost immediate wall, which means he's busy, like maybe he's on the phone and can't respond. I can send him a text, and he'll get back to us in a minute." She let out a breath, and he huffed. "Look. That's not unusual. You do it all the time with other people. You just don't realize it. You think about calling, then get this mental note and decide to wait," he explained. "That's all this is. It's that same process you use all day, every day, without even thinking about it."

"Sure," she quipped, with a note of humor, "but everybody does that. I wouldn't have put it in psychic terms."

"Maybe it doesn't belong in psychic terms, but surely it fits within the realm of intuition, if that's a better word for you."

She looked over at him and smiled. "For somebody who doesn't talk about energy very much, you sure talk about it a lot."

"I talk about it when I need to," he noted, shrugging it off. "And I'm not sure this is the best time, but, considering you brought up Terkel and that you're getting hit by your twin brother's energy," he pointed out, "talking about it seems appropriate."

"That works," she conceded. "This definitely came out of left field."

"Do you ..." He hesitated, then waved his hand. "For want of a better way of putting it, do you have any protective energy up? Do you put up a barrier, besides that general stay-away atmosphere—which comes through loud and clear, by the way. But do you put up any protective barrier to stop things like this from happening?"

"No," she replied. "I wouldn't have anyway because I was trying to reach out to Don."

"Maybe he's reaching out to you but either doesn't know what he can do or is incredibly powerful and isn't modulating it well—"

"Or he's very powerful, and this is a getaway kind of thing."

"Maybe he doesn't have a clue what he's doing, and he's just punching out at the world because he's so angry."

"That feels more like it," she said. "It feels very much as if I got caught in some backlash. I wasn't looking for it. It was looking for me. Now, whether he's seeking somebody like me, I don't know," she added. "I think he's just …" She pondered it, then shrugged. "*Reacting.*"

"*Reacting* works. In a way we expect that from people who haven't been trained in this energy work. We need to have a certain amount of understanding as to how this energy craziness works in order to not just be sitting here and reacting," he shared, with a gentle smile. "I mean, it's not that easy to just let all this happen around you and to not question it. And questioning it doesn't mean that it won't be something that works out well, but you do have to deal with the answers. Still, if you don't ask questions, you don't have to face the answers."

"Do you think anybody really doesn't want answers in this?" she asked, staring at him.

"I've seen it. A lot of people out there are seriously angry and don't care what's going on. They're just in a red-hot haze and are lashing out. For all we know, Don could have been in a fight that just happened. Maybe he punched somebody. Maybe he hesitated …"

Sadie immediately filled in the rest of the sentence. "Maybe he killed somebody in his own crew?"

Morrison nodded slowly. "That is a possibility, especially

if they broke up the partnership, or there was some feuding, and Don took one side, and somebody took another. No telling what could have happened in Don's world," Morrison said dispassionately, and it unnerved her. "But for that energy to have blasted you like it did, it sounds very much like there was a dart of energy, a fury that lashed out, and whether you caught the backlash because you are somebody who can feel that kind of energy, or because he's very connected to you, or Don's not very good with his aim when using his energy like that, I just don't know."

"I don't know either," she admitted, staring at him. "It's not something I'd ever really considered. I was initially thinking of my twin brother as someone nice and comforting. I even imagined a crying jag between the two of us, lamenting all we missed out on together," she shared on a bitter note. "Instead, my brother is a killer, a murderer, roving around with seemingly unleashed fury. … If that's true—and I don't have any reason to think it's not—I don't even know how you can stop him." Sadie sighed. "That energy he just hit me with was brutal," she whispered.

"It was brutal. I saw it, and I saw how you reacted to it," Morrison agreed. "So that's another issue that we'll have to deal with. It's potentially possible that Don has more power than he knows how to handle or to understand, and he may not realize what he's capable of."

"Or he does know," she suggested immediately, "and he's using it against his partners. I mean, what if he's the driving force behind all this?"

"That's certainly possible, especially if he just came into some energy ability or just finally realized what he could do with it. Or maybe he hooked up with somebody who showed him what to do with it." Morrison shrugged. "I don't have answers, and it seems that all we have is more questions."

She settled back into the passenger seat and groaned. "We should have brought coffee."

He laughed. "I would suggest that we get delivery, but I don't know if they deliver to a car parked on the side of a street. Besides, we're trying to keep a low profile. So, we'll sit here and be quiet for a bit. Terk's arranging for somebody to come take our spot, so it won't be too long."

She nodded. "Tell them to bring coffee."

"Yet, if he takes our spot," he pointed out, "we need to just leave and not to draw attention to the fact that we know the person in this other car."

She sighed. "Fine," she muttered, then settled back, closing her eyes.

"I guess I'm the one who'll keep my eyes open, *huh*?"

Such a note of humor filled his tone that she opened her eyes and smiled at him. "Oh, fine. I will also keep watch," she muttered. "I was attempting to send out a signal to see if I could find Don."

He looked at her intently. "And?"

"You interrupted me," she said, closing her eyes again.

"Don't let me do that," he told her. "Anything you can find would be a help."

"Got it," she muttered.

And, with that, she settled back into her seat a little bit more and sent out a probe, looking for the same energy that had hit her. She didn't know how to do what she was doing, so she just went on instincts, which, as far as anybody could tell her, was all they were doing anyway. Kind of weird to think so much ability was out there, yet nobody had names for it, training for it, or even an understanding of it. If you have a body, a physical human body, then who knows what all else was possible because nobody really explored it. Well, except for the elusive Terk and also Celia.

So here she was, with her mind calling out to her brother, *Hey, Don, are you there?* She kept calling out to him, but she got absolutely no response. She did it again and again. She sagged into place, then looked at Morrison with a shrug. "Nothing."

He nodded. "Leave the door open, just in case."

"As long as he doesn't punch me the way he did before," she muttered. "I can't tell you how much that hurt and still does."

"He's not likely to be punching you individually as much as hitting at any available target."

"I get that. I just don't really want to have a repeat of that."

"Understood," he noted, with a smile. "Now, how about we take our leave and maybe we can go get some food," he asked, with a smile, pointing at a vehicle that just drove past them.

"Who's that?" she asked.

"It's Gage."

"Oh, good, we get to leave."

His phone buzzed then, and he looked down at it. "Gage is in position. So, yeah. We get to leave." He started up the car and slowly pulled out.

As they drove past, Sadie smiled at Gage, who gave her a quick grin. Once they had driven out of the immediate area, she asked, "How about some coffee and a whole lot of food?"

"Good idea. Any particular place in mind?"

"Yeah, the one where I caught some energy before."

"Fine," he said, looking at her. "I didn't realize you were

still catching energy."

"The thing is, I guess I wasn't realizing that's what I was catching," she muttered. "Now I'm questioning everything since this all started."

"That's a good idea, and, if you come up with anything, you need to tell me," he muttered.

"Will do, except that it seems way too easy."

"Not necessarily. Let's go to this spot you found, and we'll see what we come up with." They pulled into the parking lot of a small café, and she smiled in delight.

"It's an Italian place, with outdoor eating spaces," she noted. "I always wanted to try one of those."

"Can't say I've tried one myself," he muttered. As they hopped out, he reached out a hand, and instinctively she placed hers in it.

She looked down at their entwined fingers. "Why?"

"Why not?" he asked, with a laugh. "It just seemed to be the thing to do."

"Yet I responded as if it was the thing to do as well," she noted, shaking her head. "That's very *not* like me."

"It's not a case of it *not* being you versus something else," he pointed out. "Why can't it just be natural?"

"It should be just natural, but it feels weird."

"Meaning it's not behavior you're used to."

"Right. It's not something I would normally do." She shrugged, and they walked inside the café, finding a menu board up. He sized up the menu, as Sadie looked around. Then she froze. She nudged Morrison and whispered, "Look who's behind the counter." He turned to the other side to see a young woman, who he recognized full well as Penny.

He nodded. "So, that explains the energy coming from here. I can feel it too."

She sighed. "So now what?"

He smiled. "We eat and drink and don't say or do anything." She hesitated at that, but he squeezed her fingers and nodded. "It's important. It keeps you safe, and it doesn't somehow alert your brother."

MORRISON APPRECIATED THE fact that Sadie was at least following instructions, knowing she was studying the other woman intently. When their order was ready, he got up, left Sadie at the table, and headed to collect their food and drinks. As he walked back, Penny stepped up to the counter and helped another customer. Her voice was soft, gentle, and other than that, he couldn't tell a whole lot about her.

As he walked back over and sat down, Sadie whispered, "A lot of my brother's energy is hanging on her."

"I imagine there is, what with her being the crew's getaway driver."

"*Right.*" She winced and nodded. "How do you ever learn about all this stuff?"

"Through people like Celia and Terk. Celia's his wife now. I thought you participated in one of her research studies."

Sadie nodded. "Yet it was more of a one-way endeavor. Celia gathered information from us, but she wasn't so keen on divulging anything to us. Plus, maybe I wasn't as gifted back then." Sadie shrugged.

Morrison snorted. "Celia's always after anybody who comes through there to give her permission to examine them."

Sadie pursed her lips. "I would love to be her research

assistant. Wouldn't that be a fascinating job to do?"

Morrison shook his head. "As far as I understand, most of Terk's own team members aren't terribly thrilled to work with Celia," he said, with a laugh. "You also have to remember that everybody who does this is learning as they go and doesn't necessarily want to share anything about it. It's dangerous to share, and it's dangerous to have people know too much. We cannot let people in, not when there is the CIA, MI6, and KGB on our asses."

"Back to that whole fear factor, *huh?*" She picked up her coffee and sipped it, then nodded. "I guess I can understand that. After all, I don't have any answers to all the questions you guys keep asking me."

"And yet you're the one who contacted us, so the questions need to be answered, one way or another." When she glared at him, he shrugged. "I get it. You don't want to be reminded of a lot of this, but the fact of the matter is, ... somebody out there is killing anybody who gets in their way." His voice had risen slightly.

At that moment, Penny walked over and wiped off a nearby table and smiled at him. "You know it would be nice if everybody tried to focus on the positive in life instead of the negative."

He nodded at her. "I absolutely agree with you. I don't know if you heard but there was another jewelry heist this morning."

She paled and shook her head. "I didn't know," Penny whispered. "I'm so sorry. That's terrible."

Sadie added, "Even worse, they were literally just trying to do their jobs. I'm not exactly in the market to buy jewelry," she noted, with a wry look, "but I would think that any jewelry store would close down rather than try to stay open and end up with this happening."

"You also have to think about the people who are doing these crimes," Morrison added, studying Penny intently. "I mean, what does it take for somebody to have such a lack of compassion for human life that they would shoot the security guard over some jewelry?"

"Oh, I agree," Penny muttered, staring around. When another customer walked up to the counter, she scrambled. "Excuse me," and headed back over.

He looked back at Sadie. She nodded and whispered, "That's interesting. It's almost as if she has no idea."

"I'm pretty sure she is getting some idea now," Morrison suggested. "Did you read her energy?" Sadie's frown indicated that she obviously wasn't understanding, so he went on. "I think she may remember how she drove three men to that location. It will be a shock when she finds out she is connected to it. Maybe not directly, but she is connected."

Sadie winced. "Still sucks though."

"It absolutely still sucks," he agreed.

Sadie sighed, picked up her sandwich, and started munching.

Morrison asked, "Can you feel Don's energy around her now?"

She looked over at Penny and frowned, then closed her eyes. "Yes. I do."

"Well, as her part-time job requires, Don would be in the vehicle with her."

Sadie shrugged. "It's sad because Penny probably just thinks she's providing a ride, earning something on the side. ... It certainly takes a lot of money to raise a child today." Remembering what her twin brother had just done, her shoulders sagged again.

Morrison nodded. "Still not sure he's guilty of the shootings, but we do need to keep a lid on the optimism."

She winced. "I didn't even think I was such an optimistic person until all this blew up," she muttered. "Who knew that so many things were in the world out there that you don't even know about but are ready to turn your life upside down in a second," she muttered. "At times I think I would be a whole lot better off if my mother hadn't told me about Don."

"Yet I think the truth is always something we're better off knowing," Morrison shared. "I get that not knowing would allow you to avoid dealing with this next stage, but, in the end, you still know more about your family, where you came from, and what happened. Thanks to your adoptive mother, you can seek out more information, versus your adoptive father who just didn't want to deal with it."

"I don't know that he didn't want to deal with the issue," she clarified, looking contemplative, "or whether to him it was just a done deal and not one that required reopening. He always had a very simple outlook on things, so, to him, it was probably not an issue."

Morrison chuckled at that. "And he probably slept a whole lot easier by looking at the world in that way." By the time they finished eating, she was ready to go. He looked around and asked her, "Now where do you want to go?"

She shrugged. "I don't know. I feel antsy. I feel like …" She stopped, frowning again, looking at him with an odd expression.

He gripped her hand, feeling the energy flare between them. "Talk to me," he said, his voice low.

"I feel like going for a walk," she whispered. "Yet it's not *my* feeling." His eyebrows shot up, and she shrugged. "I feel as if he's close by, but I don't know who *he* even is."

Morrison got to his feet, then still holding her hand, he half supported her, sensing a certain amount of weakness in her knees as she stood up. He whispered, "Let's walk out of here. Maybe he's coming here."

"I don't think so," Sadie muttered.

Still, they walked slowly outside and out there she collapsed onto a nearby bench. "All of a sudden my knees are weak," she whispered.

"Oh, I got that," he confirmed. "I'm just trying to figure out why."

She closed her eyes. "I don't know why, but …"

He wished she would stop trying to formulate a logical response and just give him the information that was in her head, but it was likely such a shock to her every time something came through that she was trying to process it each time. "It's easier if you get out of your own way," he stated, taking a firm tone.

Finally she opened her eyes, stared at him, and gave a broken laugh. "And that shouldn't make sense, but it does," she declared, with a headshake. "I can't even imagine what most people would say right now."

He sat down beside her, looked around, and began, "So, this instinct to go for a walk."

"I still feel it."

"Is he outside walking?"

"No, he's contemplating it. No, it's more than that. It's as if he's pacing, as if he wants to go out for a walk but isn't sure if it's a good idea."

"Okay, do you get a sense of direction? I mean, are we going toward his energy?" he asked, with a hand motion. "Or is the energy coming from behind you or to the side of you? Where is it coming from?"

Her arm immediately pointed to the left.

"Okay, let's go for a walk then," he said, with a smile. "Even if it goes nowhere, it's still good for you to walk."

She rolled her eyes at that but got to her feet. "Unless I collapse after my knees go weak, like they just did."

"I'm presuming that is because of his thought processes."

"I don't know what it is," she muttered.

"Let's go find out." Morrison hooked his arm through hers, and they started walking in the direction she had pointed out. They hadn't gone very far, maybe ten steps, when she suddenly sat down on another bench.

"Is he sitting down?" Morrison asked her.

She frowned at him and nodded. "I think he is."

"But you should be able to stand back up again, right?"

Frowning, she stood back up and nodded. "Okay, I can do that." Yet she flopped back down again. "But this is …"

Morrison laughed. "It is a lot of things. *Bizarre* is a term that comes to mind, but don't worry about bizarre, don't worry about any of it. Let's just keep walking in whatever direction that energy is coming from." And, with that, he got her back up on her feet and nudged her forward.

# CHAPTER 7

SADIE UNDERSTOOD WHAT Morrison was trying to do. He was shifting her focus to use this energy flow in some way that was constructive and helpful, but to feel her body almost trying to follow commands from somebody else was the strangest thing she'd experienced yet.

She walked several more steps, and Morrison slowly kept pace with her. She muttered, "I feel as if I'm recovering from some injury. I am so sore."

"That's how you look too," he noted cheerfully, "but that's okay. You don't care how anybody else views you."

"*You* don't anyway," she said, with a smile.

"Neither do you, not really," he clarified in that same gentle tone she'd come to understand from him.

"You're being very considerate."

"I'm a very considerate person," he noted, frowning at her. "Did you think I wasn't?"

She shrugged. "I'm not sure what I thought. It's just … I need to keep this up and to figure out what's happening. … It seems he's up and pacing again," she added suddenly.

"Good, let's go forward as fast as we can, so we can get as far as we can in his direction. That will probably trigger another surge of energy because you'll pick up a stronger message from him. Yet hopefully we'll get close enough that we can pinpoint where he is."

"I think he's back in that same apartment."

"Good, let's get there faster." They kept walking, and, when they came around the corner of the block, she smiled.

Sadie pointed. "It is the same apartment."

AND UP AHEAD, although they had come from a different direction, Morrison could see the building. He quickly texted Gage that they were approaching from the other side and that she was picking up movements from inside the building.

When Gage phoned him immediately, he asked, "What movements?"

"She's connected on a physical level to Don. When he gets up and walks around, then she is walking around, but when he throws himself down onto a couch or whatever it is that he's sitting on, she basically comes to a stop and has to collapse too."

Gage burst out laughing. "What the hell? Jeez, I'm not sure why I laughed, just being an inconsiderate bastard."

"Yes, you are. But I know, I get it. I know it sounds weird, … and don't get me started on how it looks," he stated. "All I can tell you is, we're outside, walking from the little Italian place, heading up to the apartment building. I'm trying to get her as close as we can to see if we can pinpoint exactly where Don is in there because she's connected on a level I've never seen before. She doesn't know how to control it or what to even do with it, so we're just trying to go with the flow."

"I'm coming around to your side," Gage noted.

"Yeah, you won't have any problem recognizing us. I'm

just trying to figure out how to get her to judge where Don is in terms of which floor and maybe which apartment. Any suggestions you have would be gratefully received."

"I'll be there in five." And, with that, Gage ended the call.

Morrison looked over at Sadie. "Gage is on his way. He wants to see this."

"What? Am I a show pony now?"

He laughed. "Hey, in this business, none of us have seen everything—or enough to *not* be curious," he pointed out. "This is a first for him, and it's certainly a first for me."

"It's definitely not what I was thinking about doing today," she muttered. "I was trying to reach out to my brother, but I didn't expect to lock on to him like this. I guess I don't even know if he's locked on to me or if I've locked on to him. However, if he's locked on to me, I don't think he's aware of it."

"Sure, how many are?" he muttered. "Just think about it. If you were trying to explain this conversation, how many people would even understand what you were saying?"

She laughed. "God, it's a good thing I can still laugh," she muttered, as she suddenly sat down hard on the grass. He quickly directed her to a little sidewalk and a makeshift bench. "We'll have to find places where I can sit all along the way," she muttered. "This is ridiculous."

"It's definitely unique," Morrison said. "And I've got to say, I'm not against this if it works."

"I don't know what's working though," she clarified, looking over at him. "That's the part that I don't get."

"I know, but we're getting somewhere, and you're still connected, so any closer we can get will help us in understanding how high up in that apartment building Don is."

"Right, I guess we need to cut the numbers down, don't we?" She studied the building up ahead. "It's pretty big, isn't it?"

"It is, as apartment buildings go, plenty big, and it could definitely cost us some time and a lot of issues sorting through the records for all the people there, particularly when you think of sublets and friends of friends."

"Right. Okay, let's go again. He's up."

"Why the hell is he up?"

"I don't know," she admitted, with a shrug. "It's almost as if we're back to that pacing. He wants to leave but doesn't think he should. He's afraid of getting caught, yet wants to get out and just … run."

"Interesting," he murmured. "Any other insights?"

"He's angry, very angry, … mad angry. Something didn't go according to plan, and … wait. It was supposed to be their last job, but it's not. And now he wants out because his instincts are telling him to run."

"Makes sense," Morrison muttered. "He's close to getting caught and instinctively knows it, so he's trying to do what he can to get away from it."

"And yet"—she frowned—"I'm getting a really weird sense that it's not his fault."

"Sure, but don't forget. If you're in any way connected with a crime gone wrong, and somebody dies, then, in the eyes of the law, it's still on you."

"Right, and I don't think Don thought of that," she shared. "I think he was hired to do part of the job, and the rest of this isn't going the way it was supposed to."

"And yet this isn't the first death related to their crimes," Morrison pointed out.

Sadie froze. "The connection's gone. Nothing else in

there, at least nothing I'm getting right now."

"There should be some thought process behind his leaving the heist crew. Don just might not be considering that right now."

They walked normally for a few more yards, and then, almost in relief, she sighed. "Some of the energy is easing back."

"Easing, as in he's leaving?"

"No, easing, as in he's calming down. He's calming down, and I'm still connected. I can sense that some of his panic has eased back." Then she stopped and frowned. "I think he's talking to somebody."

"On the phone maybe," Morrison suggested.

"Oh, that would make sense, wouldn't it?" He nodded and headed toward the front of the building.

"I can't get into the building," she muttered, "so that won't help."

Just then Gage came up beside them. "Oh, I'll get you into the building," he announced.

It unnerved her that she didn't even notice he was that close to her. Then he walked forward, and, by the time they got there, he had the door opened. She stared at him in shock.

He just smiled as they walked into the building. She leaned up against the wall by the elevator, staring at them. "The conversation is not going the way Don wants it to."

Gage listened to her, one eyebrow raised, but didn't ask any questions. Morrison nodded at her. "Think about it though. I mean, he wants to leave. He's panicking, and he doesn't like anything about this, and, if the crew is telling him he can't leave, then it won't go the way Don wants it to go."

She stared at him and added, "He's getting more and more angry again."

"Sure he is," Morrison noted, sending her calming energy. "Stay calm, stay focused, and keep talking to us. Whatever you're hearing, whatever you think is coming from that conversation, let us know."

"He's back to being angry, how it wasn't supposed to be like this. He wants out. It's just this litany in his head, over and over again."

"Think about it. When you get upset about something, it keeps going through your head too, over and over. The thoughts just keep driving through your head, and you never have a way to get free of it with all that repetition going on. That's what he's doing."

"Of course," she muttered, understanding. "He's still not happy."

Morrison didn't say anything, just nudged Sadie into the elevator, getting her to whatever floor they needed to be on. If he could even get her to pick which elevator button to push, that would be huge. It's not that they could count on it, but they would certainly have some direction to travel. With a cheerful smile, Morrison suggested to Sadie, "Pick a button."

Her hand instinctively hit the ninth-floor button.

With that, Gage quickly pulled out his phone and started texting. As soon as they reached that floor, she stepped out, her head tilted. "He's gone quiet."

"Of course he has," Morrison whispered, looking around. "Could be that his instincts are telling him how you're on the way or that he needs to stay quiet or ..." He contemplated it a bit. "Do you feel his energy on the move?"

"No. Not on the move at all, but it definitely feels off."

As they walked down the hallway, a couple people got onto another elevator and headed down. She looked at them and kept on going.

Morrison took a look, trying to see them, but they were already closing the elevator door. He asked Sadie, "You're sure he isn't moving, right? He didn't just get on that elevator?"

"No, but there's something." She stared at him, her face paling. Then her hands grasped her chest. "Something's wrong. Something's really wrong." She broke into a stumbling run, moving as if she were drunk and had been on a heavy bender all night. She lunged from hallway wall to the opposite hallway wall. She came up against a locked door in front of her, and she pounded on it, crying out, "Let me in. Let me in."

Gage stepped forward, while she continued to pound on the door, with Morrison trying hard to keep her a little bit quieter. Other people in the hallway had opened doors to look at them. Morrison was hell-bent on trying to briefly explain to the neighbors, since keeping Sadie quiet wasn't working. "Something wrong with the guy inside."

The doors in the hallway slammed shut, and Gage suddenly had the door before them open, and they raced inside to see a young man on the floor, his hands gripping his chest, as he stared at the ceiling. Sadie dropped to his side and cried out, "Can you talk to me?"

"Help," he whispered, his voice thin. "Help me."

"We're here. We're here, and we're getting you help." She cast an anxious look back at the others, as Morrison dropped at her side and reached out to check the young man.

"The ambulance is on the way," Morrison said.

# CHAPTER 8

S ADIE DIDN'T KNOW what the hell had gone on, but suddenly she was here with her long-lost twin brother, his features so close to hers and yet different enough to be his own person, yet he was barely breathing.

"No sign of an obvious wound," Morrison shared with Gage, as they quickly looked him over, pulling his IDs from the wallet in his pocket, and taking photos of everything in it.

She sat back and looked around at the bare apartment. "I don't even think this is his."

"It's probably somebody else's, maybe a short-term rental," Morrison noted. "Was he drinking anything? Do you feel anything? Is anything around here?"

She got up and walked around frantically.

"Don't touch anything."

She nodded. "I don't see anything." Then she stopped and pointed. "A cup of tea is over here." She frowned.

"Interesting," Morrison replied. "Don't touch it. We can always get it tested."

She stared at him and asked, "Why? Isn't this just a heart attack?"

"Yeah, but how old is he?" he asked, turning to face her, and she understood his sarcastic tone. "Would *you* expect to have a heart attack at your age?"

She frowned. "Considering how upset he was, it's not shocking."

"That's an interesting point," he noted. "Anyway, I hear the ambulance. We just have to ensure there's no sign of foul play—murder or poisoning or something along that line."

She sucked in her breath, hovering over her brother. She stared at him, wondering how he could look so much like her and yet be so very different. She gently stroked his cheek. "I don't know what happened to you, but I'm so glad I found you."

He opened his eyes ever-so-slightly and stared at her. His voice faint, he whispered, "Mom?"

"No," she corrected, "not your mom, your sister."

His eyes were clouded, and there was no recognition, no acknowledgment, no understanding, and then he fell silent again.

Within minutes, the door burst open as paramedics came in with a gurney, and they began to work on Don. Sadie was picked up and moved out of the way by Gage, as she was right in their workspace. In a frozen state, she watched as they worked on her twin brother, before he was suddenly packed up and moved out. She hadn't even had a chance to talk to him again. At some point she realized that Morrison was holding her close. She looked up from the circle of his arms and whispered, "Can we go to the hospital?"

"Everybody needs to be on this one," he agreed, nodding in agreement. "No way Don will be allowed to be on his own."

"And yet," she added, "we really don't know anything about him."

"No, we don't," he conceded, looking down at her with

a sympathetic smile.

"Yet we do, right?" she muttered, with a wince.

"Yes, we do," he replied, with a clipped nod.

Gage added, "Good job, by the way."

She stared up at Gage. "I don't even know what I did, and I doubt I could do it again."

"You would be surprised that you could, and the fact that your twin brother gave you a big step up in order to track him," he explained. "Being able to track somebody like that is a skill set that a lot of people would love to have. Forget about others. I would love it myself."

"I don't know about a skill set," she muttered. "I remember tripping my way down the hallway in a panic."

He gave her a grin. "You did look as if you'd been drinking hard all night."

She laughed. "Yeah, felt that way too." Before she knew it, she was back outside, and they all stood beside Gage's vehicle.

"Hop in. I'll give you a ride back to your car."

They got a ride to the Italian place, where Morrison's vehicle was parked. Then Gage took off again. Sadie looked over at Morrison. "I guess you're still on babysitting duty, *huh?*"

"I am," he confirmed cheerfully. "Besides, we've got an awful lot going on here, and a lot of it is good stuff now. The fact that we've found your twin brother is huge."

"What if I'm wrong?" she asked, staring at him.

"You mean, that he's not your twin brother?" he asked, startled.

"No, but what if he doesn't have anything to do with the robberies?"

"Then we're no further ahead, and that would suck," he

admitted, "especially considering that we have an injured guard in the hospital as well. However, considering what you just did, how could you pick up his energy if that man wasn't your twin brother?"

"Maybe you're right about that," she conceded, "but I don't want Don to be a part of this crew, killing and stealing."

"Of course you don't want it to be him. Nobody wants to find out that somebody they have just found in their life is involved in that," Morrison agreed. "That doesn't mean we get to bury our head in the sand either." She glared at him, and he shrugged. "Just calling it the way I see it."

"And if I don't like the way you see it?"

He laughed. "That's not exactly unexpected, is it?"

She sighed. "I don't think I like your job."

"No, you probably wouldn't," he agreed. "In many ways it sucks. A lot of things we learn about people are pretty tough."

"Right," she muttered, and they were driving again. "We are going to the hospital, aren't we?"

"We are. Gage will start security on Don, and he'll fill in Terkel and the government. We'll need their support here."

"*Great*, that means the cops will be all over the place."

"They will be, and that's not our issue. What we have to figure out now is what happened to your brother, and, to do that, we need to talk to him."

"And if there was no foul play?"

"If there was no foul play, that's great. However, if there was foul play, then Don should have some idea as to who might have wanted to do him in."

"I don't suppose anybody will be interested in that teacup, *huh*?"

"I took it," Morrison admitted. "The pot is still sitting there, and, if he dies, then I'll hand it over. I probably shouldn't have taken it in the first place, but, if Don doesn't die, and it's a poisoning, we need to know. So, I'll get it analyzed."

"Do you think that jewel heist crew would do that?"

"If your brother's having second thoughts and if he's looking to be the weak link in all this, then absolutely they'll do that. It's everyone for themselves. The rest of his crew has gone down this pathway too far for anybody to have any remorse now," Morrison explained. "The stakes are higher than ever."

"Nobody will forgive them for having killed those guards, will they?"

"Nope. It's one thing if it happened once, but this crew did it time and time again," he reminded her. "There will be no forgiveness when it comes to sentencing on this one."

With that, Sadie fell silent.

MORRISON AND SADIE pulled into the hospital parking lot and parked. He got out and walked around to her side. "Come on, and remember we have to accept whatever they tell us at this point, both the hospital staff and the local police."

"Meaning they won't let me in to see him?"

"I don't know if they can. If you could prove that you are family, maybe, but another aspect would be the fact that the medical personnel will be working on Don for a while. Plus, because the local authorities are now heavily involved, they won't want you in there talking to him without their being around too."

"Will they likely think I'm involved?" she asked.

"I'm not sure what anybody'll think, but enough deaths are involved in this already that have upset people all over. So the surviving family members will ensure the cops are on top of this as much as possible. The authorities can't afford to make any mistakes. And such a mistake in this instance would be allowing you to talk to Don without somebody in there with you."

"How do I explain what we found?"

"That is something I'll leave to Terkel," Morrison said, with a laugh.

She winced. "Can he do that?"

"You might be surprised at what he can do," Morrison declared. "The fact that MI5 brought him in is already huge. But that also means anything involving him means we give no answers. Terk would just firmly shut it down or talk to Jonas and get Jonas to deal with it," he explained, "so keep that in mind. Don't go talking about what you did or how you did it because that'll just make you come across as a crazy person."

She winced at that. "Thanks for that reminder."

"You're welcome," he said cheerfully. "The motto in all this is *Don't say anything if you don't have to*, and, in this case, you definitely don't have to say anything about how you found him."

"So, we'll just assume that, because I'm his sister, I obviously knew where he lived?"

"That sounds good to me," he replied.

She rolled her eyes at that. "I would appreciate it if Terkel or somebody backs me up because if it goes sideways—"

"Not sure anybody would back you up, but, in this instance, we won't need your testimony to put your brother behind bars, which is a good thing, as long as they can nail him for his crimes."

"*Great*," she muttered. "That's not exactly what I wanted to hear either."

"No, but you already know the score, and that's just where we're at." With that, he led the way into the hospital ER and wasn't surprised to see Gage there.

Gage walked closer as they approached and shared, "They're still working on him. He's alive, but it does seem he's had a coronary."

"He's awfully young for that," Sadie noted.

"Apparently it may have been drug induced."

"Interesting," she murmured. "I presume we're not talking prescription drugs."

He shook his head. "I doubt it. I guess heart problems and drug use tend to go hand in hand."

"Wow," she muttered. "It amazes me to think that anybody would do drugs if this could be the end result."

"The drug users don't believe that it'll happen to them, that this is the end result for them," Gage explained. "Would you? I mean, you're already out for the drugs, and, assuming that everybody will say anything they can to get you off them, you won't believe the warnings anyway. The facts won't matter because you need and want the drugs," he added, with a shrug. "It's an ugly cycle."

"Maybe," she muttered, "but I prefer to think that, if Don had had a better raising, maybe he wouldn't have gone there."

Gage frowned at her and shook his head. "The old *nature versus nurture* argument covers this. Regardless, you can turn yourself inside out with that kind of thinking. So many families have done that. Remember that a lot of really good and well-raised children turned to drugs and couldn't fight it. On the flip side, an awful lot of children who had really crappy upbringings overcame their circumstances and carved out a life to be proud of. I don't know what makes one child go with the flow and another fight their way out," he shared. "If any of us could sort that out, we would be millionaires."

"And yet I don't think money matters to you at all," she noted, staring at him.

Gage turned to her and nodded. "You would be right about that. As long as I have enough for my basic needs, I don't really care. I'm more driven by injustice—lately all about government injustice," he added, with an eye roll.

She smiled. "Everything in your world is more than good right now though, isn't it?"

"It is," he confirmed, eyeing her curiously. "Are you getting any insights there?"

"I am, but I'm not sure where it's coming from, though."

"Maybe keep it to yourself," he muttered.

"And if I don't?" she teased, laughing.

"It's all good," he declared, "so whatever. I am perfectly happy with my life right now."

"And that I would agree with. I've not seen very many people who are as content as you are."

Gage smiled. "That's because not everybody has the family life that I have," he declared, with a chuckle. "I absolutely adore where I'm at, so it's not a surprise to me."

"Good for you," she said, turning her attention back to her brother. "I just feel as if Don got the short end of the stick."

Gage lifted one brow. "Maybe he did, but he didn't have

to take that stick and wield it against somebody else."

"That'll always be the thing, won't it?" Sadie asked.

"Just because he had a bad upbringing or a rough start doesn't mean he had the right to turn around and take other people's lives."

At that, Sadie felt Morrison lay a hand on her shoulder. She sighed, looked up at him, and nodded. "I'm fine, you know?"

"I'm glad to hear that. You really did a great job tracking your brother. And, before you go there, no, it wasn't a betrayal. There is no reason for you to blame yourself."

She winced. "How did you know I was thinking that?"

"It's not too hard when I see the expression on your face," he shared. "It's your twin brother, and I get it, but just think about it. You managed to find him in time to get him some medical help, to save his life. At least this way, maybe you kept him alive so he could have a relationship with you at some point, after all this is sorted."

"Maybe. Do you think he'll want one though? Particularly if he realizes that I may have had a hand in his getting caught?"

"And in keeping him alive. Remember that? He wouldn't have survived this attack without our finding him in time."

"Maybe," she whispered, wrapping her arms around her chest. "It still feels like a betrayal."

Gage looked at her and snapped, "Get over it, because sometimes people need wake-up calls. In this case it was more literal than most. Now, whether Don will use it for good or not, I don't know. It also depends on whether he's been using energy to help make his life a little easier—or to get into the criminal world. Remember that for your sake too. If that's what he's doing, that's not cool either."

She winced. "I don't know that he is, and I never got any feeling of that from him, but what do I know?"

And, with that, the room fell silent, as they waited for the doctor to come out and tell them something. Morrison stood up as the doctor approached.

The doctor held up a hand and stated, "I'm supposed to be talking to the police."

At that, two other men stood up and joined them.

"That's all four of us in one way or another," replied one of the men, a note of humor in his tone. "How is the patient?"

"He'll make it, but it appears that his heart had already been damaged from a prior silent heart attack, so his condition is not anything we want to see for someone his age, but heavy drug use will do that. He had drugs in his system and still does at this moment, so it'll be a while before we can get him cleaned up. We have the treatments started," he shared in a sympathetic tone. "It looks as if he may need heart surgery at some point, but I'll leave that to the specialists. However, they can't do anything until he's completely free of drugs anyway, so that will be a process. I understand you're also looking to establish security for him."

"Yes," confirmed one of the two new men. "He's suspected of being part of a local jewel heist gang."

"The one who's been shooting the guards?" At that, the doctor's face sank, and he sighed. "We don't choose our patients," he declared bitterly. "So, while he's here, we'll do our best for him." He looked at Sadie. "You're obviously his sister, so do you want to spend a few minutes with him?"

She immediately nodded. "I do."

One of the police officers stepped forward, and Morrison reached out a hand. "I'll go in with her." They hesitated, and he just stared them down, and then one of the men nodded.

"You'll report back, I presume?" he asked Morrison.

"Absolutely," he stated, as he looked over at the doctor. "Is he conscious?"

The doctor shook his head. "No, he's not conscious, and I'm not expecting him to be conscious anytime soon, but we've seen all kinds of things happen that we didn't expect."

At that, Morrison pulled back the curtain and let Sadie step in. Morrison immediately stepped up behind her, not giving her a chance to refuse.

She approached the bed and picked up her brother's hand. There was no movement, no sign of him noticing her being here at all. She looked over at Morrison. "How is it the drugs weren't obvious when I heard what was going on in his head?"

"Think about it," Morrison began. "It's probably *because of* the drugs that he was so anxious and worked up, and probably another hit of drugs calmed him down finally. It's not as if you were getting much in the way of words themselves, but more of his emotional reactions, right? What he was feeling at the time?"

"Right," she whispered. "It still sucks to think of somebody his age being so damaged over drug use, supposedly recreational and self-administered."

He smiled. "A lot of people in this world are dealing with drug addictions. Your brother is unfortunately one of millions."

She winced at that and asked Morrison, "Do you think they will give him the proper care?"

"Yeah, they'll give him proper care. Remember their

creed? *Do no harm.*"

"I hope so."

"That way he also makes it to trial." She shuddered, and Morrison winced at that. "I'm sorry. That was insen—"

"No," she said, immediately stopping his apology. "It's the truth. I don't know for sure that Don's even part of this crew, and that's the thing we have to sort out. I don't understand how this could all have happened with nobody knowing."

Morrison explained, "Because nobody could see past any of the security feeds that had been doctored or whatever. Plus these heists were always done at opening time. And this crew never wanted to leave any witnesses, alive or conscious. I guess the ones left alive were too scared to approach the cops—not after seeing the others killed immediately." Morrison stared at her for a long moment. "Except for you. Which is why we were brought in. Then there is also some lag in all the reported information because of the suspected energy work. We only have that because of you too."

She winced at that. "If Don finds that out, he won't want anything to do with me."

"You don't know that," Morrison said. "Right now you have an injured young man, who is obviously your twin brother, as even the doctor picked you out of a waiting room full of people," he shared, with a knowing smile.

She nodded. "It was an odd thing to be asked if I wanted to come in and see him, when the answer is absolutely yes. But still, it was good being asked."

They stayed at her brother's side for a long time, until finally Morrison spoke up. "Come on. It's time to go." She opened her mouth to protest, and he asked, "Can you sense anything from him?"

She shook her head. "No, it's as if he's not even in there."

"And he isn't. I mean, I can see that his cord is attached, but I don't think he's there very much at all. Remember what you mentioned about your mother and seeing her energy? Step back and see if you can see Don's cord."

She stepped back and frowned. "Just this very pale outline."

"Chances are, he's off doing his own thing. Whether he'll make it back sound and cognitive at the end of all this remains a question. We don't have any way to know yet, but they'll move him to another room. The staff still has to run a lot of tests and stuff. We won't stay during all that. I can push to stay a little longer, but you must have a really good reason, especially since he's not showing any signs of being awake." Lowering his voice, he continued. "You'll likely know when he wakes up."

She smiled at that. "It would be lovely if I did." Stepping back, she realized that the cops were here, waiting. She nodded. "Over to you guys then."

She walked out, leaving her twin brother behind.

# CHAPTER 9

OUTSIDE, SADIE TOOK several deep breaths and asked Morrison, "Now that you have Don, even though he's not able to talk yet, will that help?"

"Terk's team and our forensic guys are doing a full analysis on everybody in his circle right now," he shared, with a simple nod. "So, in a way, yes, and hopefully enough that we can get to his known associates. We're also inputting his physical measurements to run against some of the street cams to see what else we can find and who was with him at various times."

"Right, even now I hope his apartment building has cameras."

He nodded. "They're on that too."

"*Great*," she muttered, as she walked closer to him. "So, what are we doing now?"

"Going back to your place," he replied, "and either we'll stop for groceries on the way or we'll order in. In case you hadn't noticed, it's quite late in the day already."

"I noticed," she agreed, "and I'm pretty beat."

"So, what do you want to do? Go out for food, pick up food, or order in?"

She considered it. "Maybe just pick up groceries and cook?" He looked at her in surprise. She shrugged. "Something comforting, like pasta maybe."

"Good enough," he said, hiding his grin. He led the way back to his vehicle, where she quickly took the passenger seat. As they headed to the grocery store, she was already yawning. "Will you make it long enough for pasta?" he asked her.

"If we do something simple, yeah," she muttered. "But now that Don's in the hospital and seems to be safe, I'm really exhausted." They made a quick trip into the grocery store. By the time they were back in the vehicle and headed home, it had seemed as if only a few minutes had passed. "I can cook when we get in," she offered.

"I'll do it," he noted. "You're obviously exhausted."

At her apartment, they headed up to her place, with Morrison carrying the one brown paper bag with groceries in it. She stopped outside the elevator and looked back, then frowned at Morrison. "Those don't seem to be any of Terk's men."

"You're just noticing them?" Morrison asked.

"Are we being followed?" she asked in a low voice.

"I would say so," he replied. "I wanted to see if they try to head up the elevators with us."

"But they've already seen our faces, which means they probably know where I'm living."

"That would be my take on it too," he said.

"When did you pick them up?"

"At the hospital parking lot." He shrugged it off. "Terk's been alerted. Now the question is, what will we do about it?"

"Shit," she muttered. "I just wanted to go home, collapse in my chair, and relax. They picked one hell of a time to interrupt my plans."

"We can still try that, but I suspect we'll get company very quickly."

She stiffened. "Do you think they're part of the jewelry heist crew?"

"I'm not sure," he told her, "but I don't like anything about this."

She stared at him. "There's a rear entrance, so we could just head out the back, grab a cab, and go somewhere else."

MORRISON NODDED. "I was just about to make that suggestion." He nudged her forward and around the corner. A set of security mirrors high up on the walls let Morrison watch as the two men walked in through the front door, hopefully not seeing Morrison as he led Sadie quickly in the opposite direction. As he got to the outside door, he looked back but saw no sign of them.

"They'll be at my place already, won't they?" she asked.

"They are by now, yes. I suspect, if we give them another few minutes, they'll come back out again."

"Now I can't go back home because, if they know I'm there, they'll just be on my case all the time. This is a nightmare."

"Agreed," Morrison stated, as he led the way out. "We can't use the same vehicle now either." He quickly phoned Gage. "Hey, we need a pick up. We were followed back to her apartment."

"Be there in five," Gage replied. "Keep walking down the street. I'll find you."

And, with that, Morrison led her around the corner to another side street. At the end of that, they just kept walking. "Where are we, and why are we here?" she asked, looking up at him with a puzzled expression.

"Gage is coming to pick us up, but we don't want to be where we're expected to be," he explained, his senses on high alert.

"I can't believe that anybody is following us now," she noted, and then she stopped. "Those men weren't cops, were they?"

"If they were, they didn't announce that, nor tell us that they were on guard duty, so that always makes me suspicious. From what I saw in the mirror, they are probably part of your brother's crew."

"Shouldn't we be trying to follow them instead?"

"Yeah, don't worry. Terk's team is already checking the street cameras, trying to ID them," he shared, with half a smile.

"Oh, I didn't even think of that."

"These guys must not be energy workers, or they would have already disrupted the energy feed to the cameras. So it wasn't them putting out the cameras at the heists," he noted. "Chances are, it's been your brother."

"How many people were involved in these heists?" she asked.

"We're assuming four, three inside and a driver."

She nodded. "So that would be my brother, these two, and potentially one more."

"Which could still be the driver, which is Penny it seems."

"Oh, crap, I didn't think of that."

"At least we got out the back way, and we're still walking," he said. "As long as nobody picks up that we're out here, hopefully we'll be okay, … at least until Gage gets here." At that, he shifted into an alleyway.

"Are you pulling me into an alleyway on purpose?" she

asked, her voice hushed.

"Yeah, I sure am. I don't like anything about what's coming up behind me."

"Crap," she muttered. "How come I can't see or feel anything?"

"Because your energy is tuned to your brother right now, not necessarily to anybody else," he suggested in a hush. "You seem to place family over everything."

"Of course, for me it has been everything. It isn't for you?"

"No. Right now it's all about security, and that security has definitely been compromised. It feels as if we're being hunted, and I want to ensure that nobody finds us."

# CHAPTER 10

MORRISON AND SADIE stayed in the alleyway until his phone buzzed, and then he nudged her forward down the way they had come. "Gage should be here soon."

"Yeah, says you," she muttered, feeling jittery, her hand gripping his. "It's not exactly an easy scenario right now."

"You're doing fine," he noted encouragingly.

"Maybe, and yet what you mentioned resonated with me. It's always been about family. I've been so appreciative of my family—the one that I knew of, my adoptive family—that I've focused on them and done what I could for them. Yet I never even knew about my twin brother, until I was told that I had one."

"What? So now you'll blame yourself because you didn't know?" He spoke with a half-joking tone, hoping to lighten her mood.

"But I have this gift." She snorted at that. "And he's my blood brother, my twin. Isn't there supposed to be some special bond between us?"

Morrison nodded. "First, you need training with your gifts. Terk can help you with that. Celia too, I presume. Second, as for the innate twin bond, I do think there is something to that. But, again, if you didn't know you were a twin, would you recognize any hints of that bond beforehand?"

Sadie frowned, then nodded, as if cutting herself some slack on these two points.

As they slowly came out from the shadows of the alleyway, Morrison saw Gage parked right at the end, and they quickly hopped into the back seat of his vehicle.

After pulling around the corner and taking off, Gage turned and looked back at her. "You guys okay?"

"We're okay," she said, "but somebody obviously found my place. I just don't know how they knew it was me."

"Chances are, they either saw you at the hospital, at Don's apartment, or on the news." He gave them an eye roll in the rearview mirror. "FYI, you guys hit the local TV and radio stations."

"*Great*," she muttered.

"Our two tails could have easily talked to the neighbors at Don's apartment as well," Morrison suggested. "So, it's not as if there weren't options for people to find us."

"I just wish they hadn't," she stated. "I guess I was thinking that nobody would know.'

"In this world, just as we're tracking everybody else, other people are often tracking us," Gage pointed out. "Don't ever assume that you are hidden just because you're not looking to be found."

TO SADIE, GAGE'S words seemed prophetic somehow, but she didn't quite understand how to make good use of them in this circumstance. She realized that Gage had seen and had done many things in the world, but he had obviously seen more than just the commonplace to have wise nuggets like that. She should be paying greater attention to her surroundings, yet all she wanted right now was to be back home, safe and sound, not having gone down this pathway at all.

Morrison squeezed her hand gently. "Don't allow regrets to enter your mind. You do what you can and leave the rest to others."

She winced and nodded. "It keeps coming back to that, doesn't it? I don't really give a crap about the stolen jewelry, if they hadn't started killing people—"

"Exactly," he agreed. "Of course law enforcement can't take the same viewpoint, but, once the killing starts, it's a different deal, and that has to stop."

"I wonder if Don even realized it would get violent."

"Too often nobody realizes that, but the minute somebody brings a weapon to a robbery, there is a really good chance of it going sideways very quickly. Most people think, *Well, I didn't have anything to do with that part, so I won't pay the price*, but it does matter because of the involvement in a felony at the time. So, everybody is involved, even the driver sitting outside in the car in most places around the world. That's how you end up with multiple people serving time for the same murder."

She nodded. "I get that. I really do. I just think the whole thing sucks that I've been brought into this." When they pulled into an underground parking lot, she looked out the car window and asked, "Where are we?"

"It's a hotel, so we should be fine here," Gage replied.

She studied the back of his head. "How do you figure that?" she asked, rolling her eyes at him. "Don't you think you were followed?"

"No, I wasn't followed," he declared. "And we should get inside without being noticed because we're already registered and have a room." He laughed as he ushered them both out of the vehicle.

Within minutes they were inside via a restricted entryway, and soon she was taking in their small hotel room, with a kitchenette and a small dining table and two chairs. "We're here, but now what?" she asked. "I really hope this isn't my life now."

"I hope not too," Gage agreed, "but would you rather meet up with these people in person?"

She shook her head. "No." At that she looked at Morrison. "Do you have any updates?" He in turn, looked over at Gage, one eyebrow raised.

"We're about to check in with Terk," Gage shared. "Hopefully they've been able to get faces off those cameras."

She sat down on the couch, watching Morrison put their bag of groceries on the counter in the kitchenette. "This doesn't even have a proper kitchen that we can cook in," she grumbled, mad at herself for even complaining.

Morrison suggested, "We can order in just fine right here. Or can we?" He turned to Gage again.

At that, Gage shook his head. "No, nobody is coming here, so I would rather go pick up something. I'm about to head over and check out your apartment to see if it's safe to go back. Maybe these will tide you over," he said, tossing them a package of cookies from their grocery bag. Then he was gone.

She stared at Morrison. "Somehow I feel as if I never quite know what's happening next when Gage's around."

Morrison grinned. "Maybe so, but he's a good person to have in our corner, that's for sure. Plus, he knows you'll be more comfortable in your own place if we can make that happen, but don't get your hopes up yet. Let's just get through this next bit and see what Terk's team can come up with off the street cams, even off the jewelry store cams." With that, he sat down beside her and brought out his laptop.

"At least you have a laptop," she muttered.

"Don't you have your phone?"

"Fine," she muttered, pulling it out, "I guess I can check my emails."

"When do you have to go back to work?"

She frowned at that. "Not yet, I have another day off."

"You may want to ask for a couple more."

"Not exactly what I want to do," she muttered, "but whatever."

"It's what you need to do for now," he stated, "because we don't want anybody heading to your work, looking to cause you trouble there."

"Oh, crap. No, that's not what I want either." So, she went through her phone, checking on everything. When Morrison sucked in his breath beside her, she looked over at him in dread. "That doesn't sound like something I want to hear."

He grimaced. "They've identified both men who went into your brother's apartment, right before we got there." He frowned at his laptop screen.

"It doesn't seem you're happy about it."

He made a few more clicks on his laptop and brought up pictures of the two men.

She leaned over to study them and shrugged. "I don't recognize either of them."

"No? Maybe you better take a closer look at this one."

She stared at it for the longest moment. "Something is definitely familiar about him, but I don't know what." She frowned, checking it out again, then turned to Morrison, catching the odd look in his gaze. "Okay, obviously you're seeing something that I'm not, so what the hell is the deal?"

He took a slow deep breath, made a few more clicks, and brought up a photo of her twin brother, Don. After another few clicks, Morrison brought up the photo of the one man he'd been talking about, with both pics side by side on the screen.

Then her heart slammed against her chest. She muttered, "They definitely share similarities."

He nodded. "What are the chances that you have more than just a twin brother and may have an older blood brother as well?"

With that, her heart almost exploded with pain as she whispered, "Are they both criminals?"

He slowly nodded. "I am afraid to say so, but that's what it looks like."

MORRISON STUDIED SADIE'S facial expression yet again. He knew it had to have been a terrible shock, and he had been hesitant to bring up the similarity of the two faces, but, when she hadn't seen it right away, he realized it had never occurred to her that she might have more family out there than just a twin brother. But the thought that both brothers might be criminals was a bit more than she was able to handle at the moment. She sat in the corner of the hotel room couch, a blanket tucked up around her, not sleeping and yet not really awake, certainly not willing to deal with the world.

Morrison got up, walked closer, and she gave him a

small smile. "I'm okay."

"Are you?" he asked. "You don't seem to be." She shrugged. "I know that finding out you potentially have yet another sibling must be hard."

"I guess it's possible, but he could be a cousin too, right?" she asked, looking at him with a hopeful expression.

"That's possible, and we've certainly seen families come in all variations. I would say he's at least family, possibly a half sibling. Yet, until we get more information," he added, trying to keep his expression as unreadable as he could, "it'll be hard to know for sure."

"So, what about my brother in the hospital?"

"I haven't checked in the last ten minutes," he teased, "and that's all it's been since you asked me about Don the last time." She winced, and he sat down beside her. "I'm sorry. This is not at all how we thought today would go."

She gave him a hard look. "It's not how any of us thought it would go, and it's not your fault. I appreciate the fact that you're still here and still trying to help." She sighed. "I can't imagine going through this on my own, and I wouldn't even know where to start. I mean, … as you can tell, I'm pretty stunned at this latest development. A possible second brother seems crazy," she admitted, as she shook her head, maybe to get rid of her thoughts, "but now I can't help but wonder if there could be more."

"That's a really good point," he noted, "and we'll do our best to get answers for you, but, as you know, it will take some time."

She nodded. "It all takes time," she muttered, "and sometimes it takes too much time. I want answers, and I want them now, but the person who I could have gotten answers from … isn't even alive anymore," she said bitterly.

"You also have to accept that your adoptive mother may not have known everything. It's very possible that she didn't know about another sibling."

"I want that to be true," she replied. "I really do."

"Maybe the two brothers were together, or maybe they were singled out as being more of an issue than we thought," he suggested. "We can't know what's going on at any one time on these matters. Just try and wait until we get additional information."

She took a deep breath and let it out very slowly.

He noted, "You've had a lot of coffee."

"No, I haven't," she countered. "This was just too much, too soon—and, by the way, one can never have enough coffee." She shot him a look. "You want more?"

"Sure," he agreed, "although I was thinking you might need food, as in real food."

She winced. "If you are referring to the cookies, I've only had a couple." When he looked at her in complete surprise, she smiled, then stopped. "What?"

"You finished the package," he stated bluntly. "So, the sugar picked you up, and now it's dropped you."

She winced. "There goes my waistline to boot."

He snorted. "Definitely don't worry about that right now. Besides, you don't ever need to worry about it. You're perfect as you are." From the expression on her face, she didn't seem to receive his simple compliment. Yet it had been so natural for him, just the way he spoke. Thankfully she left it alone, but she did get up and walk into the kitchenette, which had a small office fridge and a coffeemaker with cups, plus a few plates and plastic spoons and forks.

"Are we even allowed to leave?" She turned and glared at him. "Am I a prisoner?"

His eyebrows shot up. "No, you're not a prisoner. We're just trying to keep you safe, while we figure out what's going on."

"Are you trying to keep me safe or are you trying to keep me away from my family?" When his breath came out in a *whoosh*, she immediately closed her eyes and reached out a hand. "I'm so sorry," she muttered, shaking her head. "That was a bitchy thing to say."

"You're obviously on a turntable of emotions, so the best thing you can do is just relax as much as you can. Maybe it would help to find something to distract you, while we wait for further information," he reiterated.

She stared at him and then slumped into a chair at the nearby dining table. "I hear you, and I know that's the thing to do, yet it just feels so wrong."

"Wrong in what way?" he asked.

She pondered that. "Are you wondering if it's an energy thing?"

"I'm wondering all kinds of things right now," he declared. "One of the things we have to consider is this. ... When you felt all that energy, did you feel one brother or—"

She sucked in her breath. "Or the other. Exactly, but if we are twins, ... I assumed that's why I recognized Don," she said, looking around frantically. "How is it that I would *not* know the difference between him and the other one?"

"Because you don't know who and what you're dealing with at the moment," Morrison replied. "None of us do."

"Would I really pick up on the other one, even if he's only partially blood related to me?"

"Absolutely," he said. "Sometimes we just have connections to people. We don't always understand how or why, but the bond seems almost unbreakable ... because it feels that way."

She stared out at the living room, her back resting against the dining room chair. "It makes sense, but right now my mind is totally glommed on to, *What if there's more family? What if this second guy is also my brother? What if there's, say, four of us? Would I not recognize that energy?*"

"Maybe you would," Morrison suggested, "Maybe you *did*."

"But that will make me question everything I've felt all this time," she wailed. "Maybe I sicced you on Don, and it wasn't him at all."

He stared at her, then just waited for her to process what she'd just said. He had mentioned that before.

She closed her eyes. "But that isn't true, is it?"

"I don't think so, but remember that, because of you, Don is still alive. We don't know who did what to him yet. However, as soon as we can get that information, we will have further details to work from."

She glared at him. "You know that doesn't help."

"No, it doesn't help right now," he clarified. "Yet I'm definitely the grounding rod you need right now," he murmured.

She got up and opened the kitchenette cupboards and the fridge. "I don't know what we can eat," she muttered, staring at the interior of the cupboards.

"I doubt if anything is here. I'm sure the hotel clears out any foodstuffs left behind by the previous guests," he explained. "Gage will return pretty soon."

She stared at Morrison. "I thought I was supposed to find something to do."

He smiled. "If you can, that would be great. I just don't know how you are doing in terms of being tired or hungry or just disoriented."

"I'm feeling very disoriented, as you well know." He just nodded but didn't say anything. "And I'm not trying to bite your head off. I'm sorry. I seem to be doing that again. I'm working off automatic reactions now."

"I know that. I really do. The bottom line is that we need to find something to do until we have more to go on." Just as he went to take a look out the window, his phone rang. He glanced at the screen and stepped into the other room. "Terkel, what's up?" he asked.

His tone brisk, Terkel asked, "Is she listening?"

"No, but she's not far." He turned to see that she had followed him. "She's right here beside me now. What's up?"

"Put it on Speakerphone."

He immediately did as Terkel asked.

"Sadie?"

"Yes, I'm here," she replied. "What did you find out?"

"You have two other siblings," he shared, "one brother named Darren, plus you have a sister."

Morrison reached out to steady her. "Hang on, Terkel. She's collapsing." He quickly moved her to the couch. "Go ahead," he added. "She's here. She's just had a bit of a shock."

"Apparently your family included four kids, two boys and two girls, who are two set of twins," Terk shared. "One connected to you and one connected to Darren. Your sister's name is Tammy. We don't have any confirmation at this point that she is alive, but we're looking into that right now. Apparently your brother Darren is here in town."

"Which is the one who we saw earlier, one of the two men following us," Morrison noted.

"Yes, that's our assumption. We obviously don't have

any DNA to confirm that at this point in time, but he is a known associate of Don's," he added. "Don, I presume, is the one in the hospital?" Terk asked.

"Yes," Sadie replied.

"That confirms the intel I have to date. That's the name he was born with. That's the name that they kept throughout foster care, though, as far as we can tell currently, he uses the nickname of Cody."

"Why Cody?" she asked.

"He's a bit of a hacker and, since he likes to code, calls himself Cody."

"What about the other brother, Darren?" Sadie asked.

"He just goes by Darren."

"I hate to ask, but is he a criminal?"

"He has a very long rap sheet," Terk replied. "So the answer to that question is a definite yes."

"And my sister?" she asked, her voice thin and strained as she stared at Morrison, the hope evident in her gaze.

"We don't have a rap sheet for her. In fact, we don't have anything," Terk admitted, his tone gentle. "Which is why we need confirmation that she's potentially still alive. We also don't have a death certificate or anything else to say she is deceased."

"Right," Sadie muttered, followed by a sigh. "Why can't you tell me that she's … a nurse somewhere, married with two kids, and having a great life?"

Terkel laughed a bit, and his tone was lit with humor as he added, "If I get a chance, I'll be more than happy to tell you that, but right now I don't live in a fantasy zone. However, as soon as I have anything more, I'll let you know." And, with that, he rang off.

# CHAPTER 11

SADIE STARED AT Morrison. "Why would foster care split up a family like that?"

"Because they couldn't adopt everybody together," Morrison stated bluntly. "It's rare for four to go at the same time to the same foster family, much less to an adoptive family. However, it's also rare for twins to be split up. I have to wonder if both boys exhibited some behavioral problems, and they both ended up in foster care for the same reason."

She didn't say anything, but that made sense. "I hate to think that I'm the lucky one who got decent parents," she whispered. "I want to think that everyone else had a chance at becoming somebody productive in this crazy world."

"Everybody does have that chance," Morrison declared. "Some definitely have a better chance at it than others, but you did not put those guns in your brothers' hands, and you need to remember that."

She didn't say anything for the longest moment as she digested his words. Then she hopped up and began to pace. "At least we're starting to get some information, so that helps."

"Yeah, it sure does," he agreed, with a smile. "I mean, think about it. You could very well have a sister."

"I did have a sister, and, maybe, if I'm lucky, ... I still will," she replied, with a small smile. "I don't know how people find out this information, but I'm grateful."

"Good. I'm sure Terkel pulled strings to get it," Morrison shared. "Though the fact that there is family involved in the shootout may have helped to open those doors."

She winced. "I'm sure if my sister knows nothing about us, it won't be the introduction to the family she's looking for."

"Doesn't matter what she's looking for, or if she's even looking," he said. "She may not even know she's adopted."

At that, Sadie nodded. "Like me. … I didn't have any idea, not until my mother shared that with me before she passed," she murmured.

"You have to at least try to understand that your mother did the best she could. Your own birth parents died in a car accident, and nobody in the extended family could keep you all. Taking on orphaned kids is a big deal, let alone four of them. Unfortunately this is what often happens."

"It sucks," she stated bluntly.

He smiled, following her back into the kitchenette. "It absolutely does, but now we're starting to get some facts, so that can only help. Why don't you get some water and try to stay hydrated. I don't know what the next shock will be, but I hope to see you in a little better shape before it comes."

She glared at him, and then she threw up her hands. "I guess I'm quite a trial, aren't I?"

"Nope, you're not, but this situation is, and we'll be in a waiting pattern for a while. We'll find out more data, but it'll be piecemeal. So you must be prepared to hear something you're *not* looking for."

"Right. Tammy may not be alive."

He shrugged. "She could also be heavily involved with her siblings."

At that, Sadie spun around and stared at him, her mouth opening on a cry.

He held up a hand. "We don't know about her yet. You just need to be open to all the possibilities and be prepared for whatever we do find."

Taking several slow, deep breaths, Sadie turned her attention to the kitchenette once again. "If nothing else, I could at least work on cooking the pasta we bought, but I can't do that in this kitchenette. I hate waiting for phone calls, but obviously this is taking whatever time it'll take." And again she opened drawers and tiny cupboards, finding nothing of any use.

After a few minutes he asked her hesitantly, "Nothing is here, is there?"

She frowned. "No. Nothing." Then she laughed. "If I was at home, I would put some cookies in the oven first and then see what I had to be cooked," she muttered. "Seems cookies are on my mind."

"Cookies are great," he noted, "but not real food, and not among our options at the moment."

"Fine," she muttered. "I'll see what's on TV." As she headed toward the couch to pick up the remote, she got a weird sense of something energy-wise. She hesitated, not knowing just what she was getting. However, after the shoulder punches she had experienced earlier, she could almost register what this was. She tried to hide it from Morrison.

As soon as he turned to look at her, he knew. "What?"

"Maybe nothing."

"Don't try to understand it or to decipher it. Just tell me what you're feeling."

"I'm feeling something," she began, "but I don't know

what. I don't know who. I don't know anything. It's just a nudge."

"Okay, a nudge is good," he replied. "Keep that doorway open."

"What doorway? Open how?" She snorted. "Honest to God, I don't even know what that means," she muttered. "It's you and your doorway talk that's more unnerving than anything."

"That's because thoughts of this being something that you could control—or not—is what's upsetting you," he explained. "Once you learn to control these nudges, then it becomes empowering."

"I'm not there yet," she stated.

"No, you're not, but that doesn't mean you won't get there pretty darn quickly. You've already shown that you have quite a good way of relating to the energy, if not understanding fully what's happening," he pointed out. "It's all about sensitivity, your sensitivity to these energy signals, so keep that connection going and stay alert. Let us know if anything else changes."

MORRISON WASN'T SURE what Sadie was up to, if anything, but he kept a wary eye on her regardless. She sat on the couch, flipping through the channels, pausing occasionally to watch a few minutes of one program, then another. "How are you doing?" he asked.

"Bored silly, but I'm not getting that same pinging," she shared.

"Pinging?" He stopped and turned to her.

"Yeah, you know, that nudge thing."

"And yet *pinging* has a very different connotation."

She turned slowly and stared at him. "Meaning?"

"Meaning, that sounds as if somebody is sending out a signal, looking for someone to respond. When your phone pings, it's looking to see if a cell tower is around close by to use," he explained. "So, *pinging* in this instance could have all kinds of interesting connotations."

"I don't think I like any of them," she muttered.

"Maybe not." He hesitated, staring at her, then asked, "And you say it stopped?"

"Yeah, it stopped, so I'm not feeling anybody."

"So, you *were* feeling somebody?"

She looked confused for a moment and then shrugged. "I know it sounds stupid, but I'm not sure what I was feeling, … if I was feeling anything," she noted, "and that, of course, is not helpful."

"It might not be helpful," he conceded, "yet anything that we can sort out right now is huge."

"Yeah, I hear you. So I guess that pinging was important then, wasn't it?"

"It was important," he agreed, with a smile. "It also means that potentially somebody is out there, sending out alerts. It could be one of your brothers trying to contact your other brother, and they're just sending a blanket echo relocation thing, or it could be Don pinging to see if his other brother is online, so he can talk to him."

She stared at him. "This whole conversation," she began, with a wave of her hand, "would get a lot of people put into an asylum."

"No doubt about it," he agreed. "It does, and has put a lot of people in asylums. It doesn't change the fact that people are out there who can connect and can contact others in that way. Terkel speaks telepathically to all of us all the time." She stared at him in shock. "We don't advertise it because it would make the world very uneasy to know a lot of what Terk can do."

"And not just him either," she noted. "Also his team, right?"

Morrison smiled. "You can ask them about that, but a lot of the team members have very interesting abilities," he stated, with a nod, "and I don't even know all of it."

"Would you want to?" she asked suddenly.

"I don't know," he admitted. "It's been an interesting deal working on a case where energy is involved. I mean, it certainly allows me to use my intuition, not that I have any abilities like they do."

"Yet you do," she argued. "I can feel it."

At that he stopped and frowned at her. "You can what?"

She shrugged. "I can feel it. I can feel when you're utilizing energy to see, to test instincts, that kind of a thing. I sense you sending out those telepathic messages. I can't interpret them. I can't listen in," she added, pondering her wording. "I can't see what the messages are meant to be, but I know when you're sending them."

Astonished, he said, "It would have been good if you had told me that earlier."

She again shrugged. "Why? It's not as if I can jump into the conversation."

"Are you sure about that?" he asked, with a note of humor. "At this point I wouldn't be surprised at anything you can do. I think you just haven't had a chance to really utilize your talents to this extent, so you don't know what you can or cannot do."

"Maybe," she muttered. "It's interesting, all of this," she

shared. "I mean, to think that there is even a field, a whole field of this stuff that we don't even know about."

"Not only a field," he clarified, "but teams who work it, teams who are actively involved in using these gifts—for the good of the world. That's what always surprises me. But, as soon as you get people on the good side, you realize they have to be there because the bad guys on the other side seem to have these gifts too."

"Right," she whispered. "That's the part I don't want to think about."

"And not thinking about it might work for a while, but, once you're triggered into energy work yourself, I don't think you can bury your head in the sand any longer.'

"I wasn't really trying to," she replied. "I didn't even know there was any sand to bury my head in."

He burst out laughing at that. "Good point." He sat down next to Sadie, trying to pass the time by watching a movie.

"Feeling better?" he asked her, during a commercial break.

She nodded. "Not quite there yet, but better." Just then she stiffened.

He looked at her carefully and asked, "Pinging, by any chance?"

She frowned and nodded. "It's almost as if somebody is calling."

"Okay."

She stared at him in shock. "You know how I feel about all this."

"How you feel about it now, versus how you'll feel about it once you have a handle on it, is a whole different story. Maybe your siblings got a handle on it a long time ago."

"Maybe," she whispered, but an off expression took over her face.

"Are you trying to contact the sender?"

She immediately switched her gaze to Morrison. "Should I?"

He shook his head. "No, not right now. I would advise you not to, since we don't know who is calling. Maybe it's your other brother. What would be nice to know is whether he's calling for Don in the hospital."

"I don't know," she whispered. "Speaking of Don, maybe it's him calling out."

"That's possible too," he noted. "Did you make any contact with him prior to this?"

"No. I wanted to, but, when I realized that he was involved in this nightmare, I just didn't know how."

"It's a good thing you didn't," Morrison said. "It keeps you separate from this whole thing, just in case the police wanted to look at you as being involved."

She winced at that. "I certainly don't want them to see me as being involved, but I highly doubt that they haven't already considered that."

He smiled, then gave her a casual shrug. "That's quite true. The government is the government. As long as they think something might be going on, they will be all over it."

"Even if I didn't do anything, right?"

"Even if you didn't do anything," he confirmed. "Not to mention that they need to rule you out, whatever that takes. You all are related, and that can only be hidden for so long."

Her face twisted again.

"Is the pinging hurting?"

"No, but I want to jump in. I want to respond or something. Something is very compelling about it."

He gripped her hand and shook his head. "Please don't, not now."

She stared at him. "But what if it's my sister? What if it's Tammy calling out to me?" She had a longing expression on her face. "I mean, maybe she's involved in all this energy stuff."

"Maybe she's also involved in these jewelry heists."

Sadie shook her head. "No, she wouldn't," she muttered, with such a positive note that he had to stare at her.

"Is that wishful thinking?" he asked.

She flushed. "I don't know, … maybe. I just feel as if, us girls, we probably got the lucky deal out of this, and the boys didn't."

"Girls are definitely adopted more often than boys," he noted, "right or wrong. Boys tend to be a little bit of a handful, particularly when they come out of some of these rough situations."

She nodded. "I don't know what it is, but …" She turned to him. "Please let me answer."

He hesitated, then said, "Let me talk to Terkel first." And, with that, he quickly picked up his phone, thankful when it was answered right away. "Terkel, we've got a situation." Then he went on to explain it, on Speaker, so she could participate.

Terkel asked Sadie, "What is it you're receiving?"

"Somebody calling out," she replied. "Not so much that they're calling out for help but almost as if they're sending out a blanket signal."

"It could be a transmitter," he muttered, "sending out a message to see if a receiver is out there."

"Yet, if I'm picking it up—"

"It just means that you are a receiver," Terk stated, "but

we already knew that because you're receiving energy."

"You mean, there's a name for what I am?"

There was a smile in his tone as he confirmed, "Absolutely. You have a bit of training to go through to understand what you can do and what you can't do with this." They both heard the smile in his tone as Terk went on. "We don't even know what all you can do yet. So far, you've been fairly enterprising, but the fact that you're picking up what somebody else is sending means that there is a good chance you can do a lot more."

"Yet this person …" She hesitated.

"Doesn't sound distressed, right?" Terk spoke in a totally neutral tone. "It doesn't seem to be somebody calling out for help."

"No, I don't get that impression at all."

"And that's a good thing," Terk noted, thinking out loud. "In this case, it would be a good thing to *not* respond, particularly as we don't know where it's coming from. Can you pinpoint a location at all? Is it coming from the hospital? Is it coming from an apartment building? Is it coming from a place you have been to before?"

"How do I tell that?" she whispered, shutting her eyelids as she considered the sound. "It doesn't sound like a voice."

"No, it'll be almost like a seek beacon," Terk explained. "Somebody out there is trying to connect with anybody—or at least somebody out on the ethers."

# CHAPTER 12

"**Y**OU KNOW HOW absolutely bizarre all of this sounds, don't you?" Sadie asked Terk.

"Yes, I do," Terk admitted. "This is the world I live in. I understand how it sounds. Give me a minute. I'll see if I can track it."

"You?" she asked.

He laughed. "Yes, I'm a receiver and a transmitter, so give me a few minutes." And, with that, the cell phone connection went fuzzy.

She stared down at it, then looked over at Morrison. "Can he do that?"

"Can he do what?" he asked, with a wry look. "With Terkel the reality is not a whole lot he can't do. He could have made that call without even involving a phone. That's one of the things about him, and, as I understand it, his skills, as well as those of the others on his team, are only getting stronger and stronger as they're all together."

"Together?"

"Terk and his team." Morrison nodded. "They have a compound where they all live together and where their headquarters are based for the work they do. They can all live and work there at the same time."

"I suppose that, if you're around people all the time who can do this," she conceded, fascinated, "it would be a big community, full of people with lots of abilities."

"Sure, and staying together has opened new doors for them, and it makes sense in a way. Your abilities would naturally strengthen as you learn from each other and develop and do things you didn't even know you could do," Morrison shared, "which is why I gather Terk has a large collection of people now on his team or in his group. I don't even know what to call it."

"A cult," she teased, with a note of laughter.

"I don't think a cult would be well received by anybody," Morrison declared, "but I can understand why some people would consider utilizing that term. However, in this case, they work for governments all over the world, helping out."

"I guess it's such a specialized field," she murmured, "that they offer skills that nobody else can."

"Until we get into something like this case, where it would appear that the bad people have energy skills, choosing to operate outside of the law."

"Right, so in order to fight fire …"

"You need fire," he added immediately. "Exactly."

She sighed. "It's really sad to think that my family members could have found another outlet and yet didn't."

"Don't judge them for it," Morrison reminded her, "at least not at this stage. When you have a chance to talk to them and to sort it out, that's a different story."

His phone buzzed again, and he looked down to see Terkel calling back. "What did you find?"

"It's coming from the hospital," he said briskly. "I suspect it's Don, your injured twin brother, and he is out on the ethers, feeling alone and calling out for help."

"And yet it wasn't a call for help."

"No, he's seeking someone in particular, while still un-conscious, probably not even aware of what he's doing. He's most likely calling out for his brother."

"Or for anybody who can answer," she stated immedi-ately.

Terk hesitated. "Yes, that's another possibility."

"Can't I talk to him? It just feels so wrong to leave him out there."

"I'll talk to him first," Terk replied cautiously, "to see if we can get him to come back to this earthly plane. I also phoned the hospital to check up on him, and he's not awake. So, if I can get him to wake up, that would move all this forward quite nicely. So, give me … at least half an hour." And, with that, he ended the call.

Sadie stared down on the phone in shock. "My brother is out on the ethers," she repeated, staring at Morrison as if that would give her all the answers she needed.

"In other words, he's unconscious, doing whatever it is he's trying to do, because basically he's lost. You're not allowed to think of that as him calling out for you."

"How else can I think of it?" she asked, trying not to get upset. "Especially when I know that he's injured and lost."

"What we don't know is who he's calling for. It could be you. It could be that part of him knows he has a twin. Or it could be that he's calling for his brother or your sister."

She nodded. "What will Terkel do?"

"He'll connect with Don and try and bring him in enough so that he wakes up. Now Terk didn't mention it, but I've heard that Terk has some amazing healers as part of his team," he shared, "so, if anybody can do anything for Don, it'll be him and his healers."

"Right, so in other words, as usual, I sit here and wait,"

she grumbled, trying to keep the bitterness out of her tone.

"Yes, and I know it's hard, and it's getting harder as you hear more and more of what's going on, but it is what we need to do right now."

"*Great*," she muttered. She stared at the television. "I don't know that I can bear to watch this another minute, and I'm sure you really want to get back to your laptop." She sighed. "You don't need to babysit me."

"I just don't want you to get so upset that you go off and do something stupid."

She frowned at him. "What do you consider *stupid*?" He hesitated, and her eyebrows shot up. "You think I'll contact *him*? I don't even know how," she cried out in frustration. "I don't even know what all this is even about or how to do any of it, and the sense of helplessness is absolutely crippling," she wailed. "I mean, if I could help Don, I just might, but I don't know how. I don't even know what's involved."

He nodded, then gently rubbed her shoulders, while she glared up at him.

Really she only wanted to sob. "I'm an absolute mess," she muttered.

"For someone who has energy skills that she has no idea how to use, you're doing great. Don't forget that."

"How can you even say that?" she asked. "I'm not doing anything the least bit helpful. It feels as if I'm on this never-ending treadmill, and I don't know how to get off."

"And getting off will happen, but maybe not as fast as you want it to," he pointed out.

She let out her breath in a hard gust and muttered, "Fine, in that case, I found a deck of cards, so let's see if you can beat me."

He burst out laughing. "I've never played cards much, so

you will beat me."

She looked at him in surprise and then in delight. "Seriously? That'll be a first. I generally suck at card games."

"That would make two of us then," he stated comfortably, "so let's see who will be the worst."

SADIE WOKE THE next morning with an odd stillness to the air, suddenly aware of that same pinging sound again. Not the cry that she had heard earlier, but this time really a *ping*, as if somebody were sending out messages. What was it Morrison had mentioned last night? Something about cell towers, looking to see if anybody out there was receiving.

For the first time, she wondered if she should avoid having anything to do with this. If it was just this broadband thing, it wanted to pick up anybody and anything, and she wasn't sure she wanted to get involved in that at all. Working with Terkel and learning a few things would be interesting, but interacting with random strangers? No way. She didn't know that she had that much trust in her soul to let just anybody into her psyche like that.

Almost immediately she felt a wash of approval sliding through her. She frowned at that and exclaimed, "What is that, for crying out loud?"

Her phone rang beside her. She snatched it up to find Terkel on the other end. "That was me," he admitted. "I was tracking the pinging that you noticed."

"Did you find out who it is?" she asked, deliberately avoiding his words that pertained to her.

"I got a location, and that's part of the puzzle," he noted. "I'm still figuring out who is doing this and what they are trying to do."

"I guess in your world they're always doing something wrong, aren't they?"

"No. We do find a lot of people who have abilities are quite lonely in life, and they have a tendency to just cry out, hoping they can talk to somebody out there. It doesn't always work out the way they want," he noted sadly. "Unfortunately a lot of people with abilities have issues and have turned to drugs or alcohol abuse to deal with them."

She sucked in a sharp breath.

"But definitely some are calling out because they're lonely," Terk repeated, "and that's why I was happy with what you told yourself about not being sure you were ready to open up and trust all these unknown people. You can't trust everybody, and just because someone might work with energy doesn't make them trustworthy. I wish I could tell you that everybody who does this is honorable and good and real," he noted in a consoling tone, "but I already know to my own detriment that it's not true."

She winced because such a harshness filled his tone, as in a *been there, done that* thing, and she realized Terk really had experienced some of the worst of what humanity had to offer, experiencing a serious betrayal of some sort. "I'm sorry. That can't have been easy."

"Nope, it wasn't, but the position I'm in now is way better than where I was, so I can find it in myself to thank those who put us here," he shared, with a note of laughter. "It's not what they expected, but when you are committed to doing good work, I prefer to think that some semblance of goodness always comes back to you," he murmured. "And, in my experience, as long as you do the best you can in difficult situations to help those with abilities, their abilities continue to grow. They continue to do more than you could even imagine," he shared. "You're welcome to come and spend some time with us and see for yourself."

Delighted at his offer, she asked, "Seriously?"

"Sure, why not?" he replied. "I seem to be collecting all kinds of people, who haven't had a whole lot of experience with abilities, or those who have had a lot of experience with their particular brand of ability but haven't had the exposure to learn what else there is to these gifts. And believe me that there is a lot more to learn. And the more we learn in our corner, the more we understand that we're not even close to tapping the potential of the psyche. So, if you want to come spend some time with us after this is over, I would be happy to have you."

"What about Morrison?" she asked curiously.

A note of laughter filled his tone when he asked, "What about him?" When she hesitated, he chuckled, a teasing tone evident in his voice. "Yes, he can come too."

"That would be lovely," she said. Then she took a deep breath. "I'm not exactly inviting him to come with me," she clarified immediately.

"That's exactly what you were asking, asking if he wanted to be there or could be there," Terk corrected, with a smiling radiance to his words. "Believe me, when you get to this stage, there really are no secrets. You see energy. You feel energy. You hear the energy, and, at some point in time, you just give up trying to hide emotions or anything else along that line. We have many solid partnerships among my team members, and they're all a big family at this point. One way or another, when problems crop up in their relationships, we know when an argument is happening. No way to hide it," he said. "Therefore, everybody works very hard at clearing their own issues, so that they don't drag other people into it."

"Isn't that hard?"

"No relationship is perfect," he noted, "but considering that you and Morrison both have abilities, … that's a hell of a good place to start." And, with that, Terk rang off.

She had barely put down her phone when someone knocked on her bedroom door. "Come in," she called out.

The door opened, and Morrison stepped in. "Your brother is awake at the hospital, and we're allowed to go see him."

She stared at him in shock for a moment and then bolted out of bed. "Give me five," she cried out.

"Five does not give you time for coffee."

"We'll get coffee at the hospital." When he stared at her in horror, she smiled. "Okay, we'll pick up coffee afterward."

And, with that, he quickly withdrew.

She dressed in double time, and, when she stepped into the other room, he was already standing at the door. She grabbed her purse, and they were outside and climbing into the vehicle he'd arranged as fast as she could make it.

"I figured you would want to go quickly," Morrison shared, "and, if the hospital was giving us clearance to talk to Don, I figured we better get there before they changed their minds."

"I thought for sure that we wouldn't be able to."

"I'm pretty sure that Gage has been working on them overnight."

"Is he there at the hospital still?"

"Yes, he's been standing guard all night," Morrison confirmed.

"Shouldn't you have gone to relieve him?"

"No, ma'am," he stated, with a smile.

"Right, so you are on guard duty over me, right?"

"If that's the way you want to look at it, yes," he confirmed. "Absolutely no way we'll let anybody else die on this case if we can stop it."

"And yet I'm not connected to the jewelry heists at all."

"No, but that doesn't mean that somebody isn't all about taking advantage of your situation, your abilities, and, for all you know, that's how your brother Don got into this."

"Oh God," she muttered, as she thought about it. "That never occurred to me. He might have been blackmailed into it." She had to admit she was absolutely thrilled to have any alternative theory as to how her twin brother had gotten involved in this mess. But chances were, Darren had brought Don in.

"I'm just throwing out suggestions," Morrison stated. "Not necessarily good ones, but there are always other ways to look at things."

"Right. … I talked to Terkel this morning."

"I heard you," he noted.

"Oh."

"Just through the doorway," he added. "I wasn't listening in on your phone call."

"No, I wasn't thinking that," she murmured. "But Terk did say that I could come visit his place and maybe learn to do more."

He gave her a big smile. "That's a hell of an offer."

"That's what I thought," she said, returning his smile. "It's a nice offer if it's something that I can make happen, though I'm not sure I can."

"When this is over with, you'll have all kinds of options ahead of you, so don't knock those down."

"No, I won't do that," she said. "It just all feels so very strange at this point."

"Of course," he agreed. "But, at some point in time, you will adjust and will become a little bit more comfortable with it, and that will make it all easier." They were pulling into the hospital parking lot when his phone rang. He hopped out of the vehicle as he answered Gage's call. "We just pulled into the parking lot, so we'll be up into the room in a few minutes."

Morrison pocketed his phone, reached out a hand to Sadie, which she quickly grabbed, then ran in to avoid staying outside too long. "Your brother is awake, and, while we'll go in and talk to him, the police will also be there."

"Right." She winced. "Don won't like that, will he?"

"Oh, I don't imagine so. We also don't necessarily have any proof that he's involved." She came to a dead stop and stared at him. He nodded, and then shrugged. "Remember?"

"What?"

"So far it's been mostly your insights."

"*Great.*" She stared at him in horror. "So, that's back to me being the reason he is where he is."

"We don't know anything about why he's where he is," he reminded her. "Keep that in mind. Whatever has happened to him, coming to the hospital, the heists, all of it, … none of that has anything to do with you. You are just relaying information—and saving his life. Remember that."

She let out her breath and nodded. "It's so easy to get messed up in all this."

"It absolutely is," he agreed, "but we just need you to stay calm, and let's go see what Don has to say for himself."

With a bright smile she walked up to see her twin brother. Only as she got to the actual doorway, seeing Gage sitting there with a smile on his face, that it hit her. She was about to go in and meet her brother for the first time, … the first time he would be lucid anyway. Then the nerves hit. "Maybe I shouldn't go in," she said suddenly.

Gage looked at her with a knowing expression. "That would be a shame, after all we've done to find him."

"I know, but now I feel as if I'm the one who found him," she cried out, "and I'm the one who's responsible."

"Did you poison him? Did you do anything to put him in the hospital?"

"No, of course not," she declared, staring at him with a frown. "What do you mean?"

"Then you're not responsible for what put him here," Gage stated.

She glared at him. "Morrison has been saying the same thing."

"Yeah, but you're ignoring him too, I guess," Gage stated, with a bright smile. "Not smart. … I get it, kind of, but right now you're nervous, upset, and worried. However, that is nothing compared to the way Don's feeling."

"Has anybody been in to talk to him?" she asked.

"Yes, the police were here earlier, and basically he's not talking."

"He might not be talking now either," Morrison noted, "but we still need him to talk."

Gage nodded. "We need him to give up some names."

"But it could also involve my other brother, Darren."

"Now that we have that name, believe me that the police are all over it, and they're trying to track both brothers' movements at the jewelry shops that have been robbed in the last little while," Gage shared. "So go on in and talk to Don, and, yes, everything is recorded, as a police officer will be in attendance as well."

"*Great*," she muttered. "How do I start? *Hey, did you know you had a sister?* Or what?"

"It is what it is," Gage stated, giving her a hard look. "Be grateful you have this opportunity."

She winced. "*Thanks* for that too." She walked to the door, took a deep breath, then turned the knob and stepped in.

GAGE GRABBED MORRISON'S arm as he went to follow her. "How is she?"

Morrison shrugged as he pondered that. "She's okay, holding up, but she keeps getting a pinging."

"What?" Gage asked, confused.

Morrison nodded. "She's receiving a ping, as she is a receiver."

Gage's eyebrows shot up. "That makes a crazy kind of sense."

"It does." He smiled at his friend and stepped into the room behind her. She hadn't moved in from the doorway, just staring at the young man on the bed. His eyes were closed. One chair was at each side of the hospital bed, one was occupied by a cop.

The cop glared at her and Morrison behind her. "I'm staying in here."

"That's fine," she replied, as she took several tentative steps toward the end of the bed.

The young man's eyes opened wide, and he stared at her. Then his eyes widened in shock. He tried to sit up and then cringed as pain racked through his body.

She quickly sat down beside him, picking up one of his hands. They didn't say anything to each other, as they both studied the face looking back at them.

Morrison felt like an intruder, as he came up behind Sadie and asked, "Don, how are you doing?"

Don swallowed hard, looked at him, then her, and back at him.

"Yes, it's your sister," Morrison confirmed. "Your twin sister."

Don collapsed back on the hospital bed, closing his eyes to digest this information.

Then a moment later Morrison saw hot tears coming from the corner of Sadie's eyes, and he felt his own heart wrench.

She wiped away her tears and whispered to Don, "I didn't know you existed until recently. I've been looking for you everywhere since then."

He rolled his head toward her, his eyes open, and he didn't seem able to speak.

"We were all adopted out, it seems, both sets of twins," she shared. "Apparently my adoptive parents had the two of us for a while. I don't understand why you were returned to the foster care system. I didn't even know this much until a few months ago, when my adopted mother passed away."

The shocks hit the young man, one after another, after another. She squeezed his hand and continued. "That's when I realized what I'd been missing all my life, what had caused that ache that never seemed to go away. It was you. It's one thing to split up children in the same family," she added, "but to split up twins?"

Don shook his head. "God, I kept having images of a, … of a little girl, but I didn't have any way to back it up or to understand who she was. I tried to reach anybody in our birth family, but I didn't have any success with that. I've never been good with red tape or paperwork or anything, and I just get angry at the people on the other end of the phone." He rolled his head toward her, his eyebrows raising up. "We have another brother."

She smiled, then nodded. "Darren. I understand we have another sister, as well. Her name is Tammy. They are twins too."

That seemed to be a complete shock to him. Then his gaze went blank for a moment, and he shook his head. "What?"

"Yes."

"I have two sisters?" Don asked.

"Apparently you have a twin, me, and Darren has a twin sister as well," she explained in a soft tone. "Our parents were killed in a car accident, leaving behind two sets of twins, two years apart. But we were all split up and either adopted or fostered to four separate homes."

At that Don started to cry, and the two of them fell into each other's arms. It was a heavy emotional moment, yet not an uncomfortable place to be. It let Morrison see the heart and soul of the young man in the bed in front of him. Morrison could also see energy flying around the room, heavy emotional wet energy, angry energy, frustration, fury, bereavement, grief, all of it in one big mixed-up mess. The cop even hopped up and walked away from the bed to come over and stand beside Morrison.

"He didn't know any of that?" the cop asked Morrison.

Morrison shook his head. "She just found out when her adopted mother passed away a few months ago," he shared. "She only found out about her other sister and brother yesterday."

"Jesus," the cop muttered, under his breath. "You would think the foster care system could do a whole lot better than that."

"The two boys didn't get adopted as far as we can tell, but both girls did."

"Of course, perfect little blond hair, blue-eyed girls," he whispered, followed by a snort of disgust. "And boys in that situation tend to be a little difficult at times, which makes sense if the report they got back on this guy had anything to do with it."

"He'd just lost both parents, had been separated from his siblings, so I imagine that wasn't easy."

"Right."

The two of them waited until the crying calmed down.

Sadie sniffled, looking back at Morrison.

He smiled at her. "So, now you have more family than you thought," he said.

She nodded and looked back down at Don. "So do you."

He nodded in shock. "I only found Darren about a year ago," he said, "and that was by accident. I was down at the pool hall, and I walked in, and everybody was teasing me, telling me how my brother was over in the corner. So I went to see this guy, frowning, yet it was pretty easy after that to figure it out," he added, with a headshake. "There is a strong family resemblance."

"Does he know about his twin?"

"No, I don't think so," he replied, staring at her. "Darren had a bad accident somewhere along the line and got a head injury, so he doesn't remember very much before then."

"So, he didn't remember me either?"

Don shrugged. "No, or me. Of course I was younger and

didn't remember him at all but"—he squeezed her hand—"I kept having these flashes of you."

"You had more than I did. I didn't even have that," she whispered. "I didn't even know I was adopted until a few months ago."

"Of course not," Don muttered. "It's easier on them if you aren't full of questions." He shook his head, looked at the cop, then at Morrison, with an oddly protective energy. "Who are you?"

"I'm her friend," Morrison stated.

She smiled, got up, and walked over to him. Just like a homing pigeon, when he opened his arms, she stepped right in and buried her face against him. He felt her body trembling, still overwhelmed by the heavy emotional onslaught.

"She's been dying to see you," Morrison shared, "afraid, happy, terrified, all of that and more. So, when she realized that Darren and another sister, Tammy, were both out there, it was quite a big shock. Just as it is for you."

Don, his gaze shadowed, stared at the cop and then back at them. "Why is the cop here?"

"Maybe we should ask you about the jewelry heists instead," Sadie snapped, suddenly turning to glare at Don.

His eyebrows shot up, and he stared at her in shock. "Jewelry heists?" he asked, his voice faint.

"Yeah, jewelry heists," she repeated, "and murders."

The color drained from his face, and he quickly turned sheer white. "How can you know about that?" he cried out. "How can anybody know?"

"Do you really think the police are stupid?" she asked, staring at him. She shook her head and buried it in Morrison's chest, as he watched the young man on the bed.

Morrison continued on for her. "It hurt her knowing

that she's just found the two of you, only to find out that you are both criminals," he declared. "She was desperate to find you, and then to find out about this?" He shook his head. "It hasn't been easy on her either."

Don stared at him solemnly. "You don't know anything about it. Apparently she had a perfect home, and she got to be a daughter and to have birthdays and to go to school and to be a normal kid," he responded bitterly. "Darren and I didn't get any of that."

"No, you may not have," she replied, immediately pivoting in Morrison's arms to glare at Don. "But that doesn't mean you had to start stealing jewelry and killing people in the process. You could have just taken the damn jewels and not killed anybody. That would have been so much better."

He shook his head. "I didn't," he cried out. "I didn't hurt anyone."

Morrison sighed. "Maybe not, but somebody in your group did, and you are all guilty of those murders in the eyes of the law," Morrison added, his tone calm. "If it's one, it's all."

"No, it doesn't have to be. It doesn't have to be. I didn't hurt anyone."

"Yet it is," the cop confirmed. "As soon as somebody dies or is killed during a felony, everybody involved is charged with the same crime."

Whatever remaining color was left on Don's face quickly drained, and he looked like a ghost.

# CHAPTER 13

SADIE RETURNED TO sit down at her brother's side. "Maybe you should explain," she urged him, "because … I need to know. I need to understand. I know that I had a better upbringing. I understand that yours was not good, and, for that, I am so sorry. Obviously I'm grateful that I did get adopted and stayed with my family, but it hurts a lot to think that you didn't get the same treatment."

He shifted uneasily under the covers. "It doesn't matter," he muttered.

"Yes, it does matter. It matters to me, but, even though I feel terrible about it, and I'm so damn sorry, I can't do anything about it—not now and not back then either. I gather that your childhood wasn't very easy."

"No," he said, staring out the window. "But whatever. … I don't need to sit here, whining about my upbringing." He snorted. "I shouldn't have mentioned it at all."

"But you did mention it, which means it's an issue," she said immediately. "And for that …" She shrugged. "Again, I'm sorry." She frowned at Don. "Maybe you can explain why this sad, bad childhood is all part and parcel of the robberies and the deaths because none of us understands. So, maybe you should explain it to me."

He shook his head. "I can't talk about it." And his voice

was low, slurred into the sheet.

"Maybe not, yet there's no way to *not* talk about it. It's not as if the police will go away. It's not as if you'll get out of here and go back to your apartment," she pointed out. "What we're still trying to figure out is whether somebody did this to you or if you did it to yourself."

He stared at her in surprise. "I didn't do anything." He looked around and frowned. "I don't even know how and why I ended up here."

"You ended up here because I found you in your apartment where you almost died," she explained. "I've been waiting for you to wake up and to get permission to come in and talk to you."

It's obvious that her words threw him. He shook his head. "No, I was at home."

"I know what you were doing at home," she said, trying to keep the judgment out of her tone. But he flushed anyway and stared at her nervously. "I get it," she added. "You're doing drugs, and life hasn't been great, and that's been your way of coping. However, whether you were doing drugs on your own or somebody gave you something that was not good, I don't know, but the fact is, you were almost dead when we found you."

He blinked at her several times, then looked over at Morrison for confirmation.

He nodded. "She's telling the truth. We found you and ultimately made sure you got to the hospital in time, saving your life."

The stunned look on Don's face revealed he had absolutely no idea what was going on.

Morrison walked closer and asked, "Any chance you got a bad batch of drugs?"

He stared at him and shrugged. "I mean, maybe. I don't know." His fingers started to nervously work the sheet.

"I know what this means," she stated, pointing out Don's twitching and nervous hankering. "That means you'll need a fix soon, isn't it?"

He winced and then nodded. "Yeah, you can say that."

"I know the hospital can give you something to help bring you down. I don't know how, but it works though," she said, "and that will be up to the doctors."

He swallowed nervously and looked around.

"No, I don't do drugs," she stated. "I don't have any experience with it."

"Of course not," Don muttered. "You're one of those Goody Two-Shoes, aren't you?"

"Maybe, if that phrase makes sense to you," she conceded. "I did go to school and all that stuff, but I didn't have a totally carefree time of it. I had a job. When Mom got sick, I stayed home to nurse her. So I lost a lot of my friends over that time period, and, once I found out about you, then that became my focus." She asked Don, "You never did find out about me, did you?"

"No, and our brother didn't know either. So, it's not as if we were looking for you," he said apologetically. "Because we didn't really remember."

"No, I get it," she whispered, feeling hurt on the inside. "But we can see each other now."

"Yeah, well, according to you, I'll be in jail for a long time, so it won't make a damn bit of difference."

"Considering I didn't have family before, it makes a hell of a difference to me."

He glared at her. "Right. As if you'll acknowledge me when I'm just a jail bum."

She frowned at him. "I guess the question is whether you're done with that lifestyle or whether that's something that you'll continue to do again," she pointed out. "It would be hard for me to work on our relationship if you'll just get out of jail and go kill somebody again."

He stared at her, shook his head. "I didn't kill anybody."

She sat back a bit, relaxed on the inside. "I'm glad to hear that much at least," she said. "It's not easy to realize you've got a family, only to find out they're all criminals."

"Is she in trouble too? Tammy?"

"I don't know," Sadie replied. "I hope not. I've never met her, don't know anything about her yet. We don't even know if she's still alive, honestly. That's something that we're tracking down right now, trying to find her."

He nodded. "It would be nice to know I have another sister," he said, immediately looking at her.

"It would be nice to know that all of us can be connected in one way or another because it's just painful to find out about each other after the fact." She smiled at him. "You need to cooperate with the police. They've been through hell and back trying to bring you guys all down before you killed even more people. And I get it. You don't want to turn anybody in. You don't want to hurt anybody else, but, at this point in time, … you're not going anywhere. You will be in police custody, either here in the hospital while you recover or in jail, awaiting trial. So you might as well do something for yourself for a change."

"Who says I'm not doing something for myself?" he asked belligerently. "You don't know anything about me. You don't get to sit here and judge me."

"I'm not judging you at all," she stated, "but, yeah, I guess I am judging you for the actions of the group."

"I told you that I didn't kill anybody."

"That's good, but it's not enough," she stated, almost losing her temper, "because, even though you haven't killed anybody, people still died, and you'll still go to jail, just by being part of the same crew."

"You've got to prove it first," he snapped, "and I don't think you can do that."

She leaned in as she whispered, "You mean, because you're using energy to scramble all the cameras?" She hoped the cop couldn't hear or understand. At that, Don's face turned beet red and then went extremely pale again, enough that she leaned forward and chastised him, "Hey, no more heart attacks." He just stared at her, then opened his mouth, but nothing came out. She turned to look back at the cop, but he was on the phone now at the far corner. She then glanced at Morrison, waiting for his approval.

Morrison nodded.

She leaned over to her brother again. "Yes, I can work energy too." He shook his head rapidly, trying to stop her from saying whatever she wanted to say, but she shrugged. "Doesn't really matter to me, but the fact that you're protecting the people who are killing people means I have to do what I can do too. So, yeah, so much for finding family." She stood up and stared down at him bitterly. "It would be so much easier if you hadn't killed anybody," she whispered. "And don't go telling me that you didn't do it. I already know you didn't, but I also know that you didn't stop the one who did."

Don stared at her in horror, then looked at Morrison, who was glaring down at him. "Jesus," Don finally whimpered.

"Yeah, a lot of shocks, isn't it?" she murmured. "For

you, for me, for everybody involved. That's not exactly the reunion I was hoping for."

Just then the doctor stepped in, looked at his patient, and frowned at her. "I think he's had enough."

She nodded. "You're right. It is enough." She gave her brother a hard look, then stepped out into the hallway, and turned at the door. "We'll be back."

As the door closed, she stopped, then leaned against the hallway wall, taking several slow, careful breaths, as she tried to get air back into her lungs. Gage stood here, with Morrison at her side, both of them staring at her in worry. She shrugged. "I'm okay. I am."

"Good," Gage noted. "What was that all about?"

"I told Don that I knew what he was doing—using energy to scramble the cameras—and that we were already onto him and that he needed to talk. He got angry at me. He is most definitely a follower," she declared. "I understand that because I am one myself. So, whoever is doing this, Don's clearly not the mastermind behind any of it."

"How is that?" Gage asked.

"It's that whole foster care or adopting thing. In his case Don's definitely got a chip on his shoulder because he grew up thinking that he would never be lovable, would never be loved. Yet at the same time he still desperately wants that connection with people," she explained. "That's him, but I don't know how it is with my other brother. I suspect Darren may be much more of a leader than this one is."

"I think so too," Gage agreed. "At least that's what our research shows so far."

She nodded. "So, how do we get enough proof to get Don to turn in the others?"

"You may have done enough right there," Gage noted.

"Did the cop hear you?"

She shook her head at that. "No, I tried *not* to let him hear, and the fact that I even knew sent my brother into a tailspin, so now the doctor's not happy with me, thinking I've upset his patient too much."

"Don also acknowledged that he was doing drugs, and it's possible he might have had a bad trip," Morrison added. "He certainly didn't suspect that anybody gave him something and would have done this on purpose."

"Doesn't mean it didn't happen though, right?" Sadie asked.

"No, of course not," he confirmed.

"What we need to do is find out who else is in the game and determine where they are," she suggested. She turned to look back at Don's hospital room.

Gage noted, "If you upset him this time, chances are, aside from the cops, no visitors will be allowed for the next little bit. The heist team could use ulterior tactics to get in to talk to him anyway," he shared, with a wry smile, "because they can't let Don go too long unsupervised by the crew."

"Of course," she agreed. "So, in other words, I might as well go home. Is that what you're really trying to tell me?"

He nodded. "Yes, and let's hope that what you told him has shaken him up enough to want to step forward and to do something right."

"I don't think doing the right things is really high on his list," she admitted softly. "As much as I hate to say it, he's spent a long time in this criminal underbelly, and I'm not sure doing the right thing is on his radar at all. I think his crime family and friends will be more of an influence than anything else, and you can almost hear them in the background, saying, *Don't open your mouth,*" she muttered.

"I can hear that. Can you too?" Gage asked, staring at her.

She frowned at him. "I just meant it as a saying."

"I know, but I can also hear it, can't you?"

She stopped, closed her eyes for a moment, then opened them again, both men eyeing her expectantly. She nodded. "I can. How weird is that?"

"That's the brother I would suspect, your other brother, I mean," Gage said, looking at her. "To have this amount of talent is one thing, but to have it run in families is another. Still, to have multiple family members on the *other* side of the law? … That's just sad."

"More than sad," she conceded, "it's devastating." With that, she turned back to Morrison. "Let's head out. I need coffee, and I need food."

"We'll go get both." He looked at Gage and asked, "Are you getting relieved?"

"I have more cops standing by to relieve me," he replied. "So maybe I'll tag along for lunch because here is my relief right now," he said, pointing as two cops came toward him. He exchanged notes for a few minutes and then rejoined Morrison and Sadie. "We're good to go."

She smiled at the cops and said, "Thank you."

They just nodded and took up positions at either side of Don's hospital room door.

As the trio of good guys headed out of the hospital, Sadie asked Gage, "Are you so good that only one of you is needed to guard Don, yet these guys aren't very good, so they need two guys to replace you?"

He shrugged. "Apparently nobody was available last night," he shared, "so I pitched in at the last minute."

"But do they need two guards?"

"Not necessarily, but Terkel is concerned about whatever abilities these bad guys might have," he noted. "So this is more of a safeguard, just in case something bizarre happens."

"Of course, *bizarre* is something you guys do very well, isn't it?"

"We absolutely do," he admitted, with a chuckle, "but then apparently, so do you."

"I'm learning," she murmured, "not very fast, it seems, but I'm getting there."

"It takes time, but, once your mind is opened, you'll find it goes very, very quickly," Gage pointed out. "What you know today versus what you'll know and understand in even a few days from now … will be a huge paradigm shift."

"It's already pretty fascinating," she shared. "I had no idea that there even were transmitters, receivers, or people who could do this energy stuff."

Gage nodded. "What we need to do is find out who is sending you messages."

"I don't think they're sending them to me, per se. I think Terkel's right, and it's more like they are broadcasting to anyone out there. Reaching out in loneliness or something to anybody really who can talk to them. It kind of breaks my heart in a way."

"That's part and parcel of what we have for a challenge in our world," Gage added. "We have so many people in this world, and only a very finite few can do this energy work. It's hard to find each other, and it's not as if a psychic directory is out there for us to sign up with."

She laughed. "Can you imagine if there were?" She shook her head. "Then again, what people can do versus what they cannot do, and what people might say they could do versus reality would make all the difference on how successful that psychic directory would be."

Morrison nodded. "And the moment you got a group like that going, you'll always get the other element, the other side of all this."

She winced. "That being another dig at my brother."

"It's not a dig at all," he countered. "It's just a reminder that life doesn't always turn out the way we want it to, just because in our minds we have a happy ending planned. Now let's go get some food, and we'll sort out a plan." So, with that, she followed him and Gage to the parking lot.

MORRISON DIDN'T EVEN bother asking where Sadie wanted to go. He just headed to the one restaurant he knew that was close by. As soon as he pulled into the parking lot, he opened the car door and hopped out, only to find her already striding toward the front door in a rush. He called out to her, "What's up?"

She turned to him, shrugged. "I don't know. I'm all keyed up, upset, have a headache. I'm stressed, not to mention so damn hungry." She raised both hands. "And I get that Don will be loyal to his family, to the one who he knows, his brother, Darren. Yet it feels so wrong to think of that as his family when he's also got me."

"But you're the new one on the block. You're the unknown element to him. Particularly once you shocked him about the energy work," he reminded her. "That means he needs to stop and reassess, and nobody likes to do that, particularly when he's in the precarious position he is in and stands to lose something big, which in this case is his freedom."

"Did he really think that they would get away with the heists and the murders?"

"As long as nobody could reveal how they were doing this, chances are they felt that nothing could be proven in court."

"Right," Sadie muttered, frowning. "So, as long as it wasn't provable, with no hard evidence against them, they felt they were in the clear."

"Unless the cops can find something substantial, such as the gun that was used."

"Which is something I don't know anything about," she noted, with a wave of her hand.

Morrison nodded. "I didn't see one in his apartment, and you can bet that was searched by the two guys who likely drugged Don."

"Of course," she grumbled.

Morrison added, "If Darren is the more dominant of the brothers, then it's possible and even likely that he has the gun." He watched as her shoulders slumped, but she didn't try to hide it. She'd come a long way in a very short time on this very difficult topic, and he was proud of her.

She'd done something that a lot of people would still be caterwauling about, but not her. She got right down to business. Even at the hospital, she tried hard to get Don to come around and to do something right and to talk to the police, and Morrison appreciated the fact that she was showing good faith, trying at least to help get this over with quickly.

Because one thing was true—currently the authorities had no way to prove that Don had even been in the jewelry store. The cops needed evidence. They needed actual forensic evidence to put away this gang, and, for that, they would either need a confession or at least some hints in a direction that would help them track down that gun used to murder people. If they could do that, it was a whole different story. But getting there? Well, … that would be a challenge all on its own.

At the restaurant, he quickly ordered coffee for them as they were led to a table and given menus. Thankfully the waitress came back right away with their coffee with a smile, then quickly left.

Gage looked over at her and asked, "Are you okay?"

"I am, but I'm really, really hungry though," she replied. When the waitress came and took their orders, she placed a very large order and continued to sip her coffee. She was edgy and a little preoccupied.

Morrison leaned forward. "You're burning through a ton of energy. Why?"

She stopped, then blinked, looking at him with a surprised expression. "I am?"

Gage turned to her and nodded. "Yes, you are. A lot more than you should be." He stopped, leaned forward, studied her closely. "I know this will sound very strange, but are you alone?"

Morrison heard him and stiffened. He hadn't even considered such a thing. He looked at her carefully from all angles, trying to see the energy around her, only to realize that she had picked up some company. He looked at her in surprise. "Now what? Damn, that's a problem," he said, looking a Gage.

"What's a problem?" she muttered, as Gage stared around the small restaurant.

"We have to fix this," Gage replied.

"How will you do that?" Morrison asked, looking over at

her, as she studied them in confusion. "She doesn't even know what she's got."

"Of course not, but somebody in her world knows, and considering that we just came from the hospital, what are the chances it was Don?"

"Oh, wow," Morrison muttered, sitting back and frowning at Gage. "It's possible. Obviously they're all doing energy work, but it would not be a good idea."

"If he is here," Gage added, "she can't be privy to any conversations."

She stared at Morrison, her gaze going from one to the other. Yet it was obvious that she wasn't even picking up on the conversation. Morrison stuck his hand in front of her face and waved it back and forth. She blinked several times and frowned at him but didn't say anything. "Do we need to get the food to go?"

"Damn," Gage whispered, staring at her as she seemed to almost be in a fugue state. "I've never seen this happen."

"No, neither have I, and I don't like it. I don't like anything about it." Morrison hopped to his feet. He caught the attention of the waitress and quickly changed their orders for takeout, plus doubled up on coffee to-go. Within minutes, they were loaded up and on their way.

Morrison drove back to the hotel. After they'd parked, Morrison pulled Gage aside. "Do you think it's safe?"

"I think it is at the moment. I think their attention is on something else."

"And yet, if we go up there, is somebody tracking her?"

"Yes," Gage replied, "another valid point." He quickly made a phone call to Terkel. "We need some camouflage."

"Okay. Why?"

He quickly explained, and Terkel's breath caught in the

back of his throat. "As soon as you get her up there, I'll come in and do some work. I'll get Cara and Clary to give us a hand too. We have to disconnect before she can't."

"Yeah, that was our reasoning," Gage agreed, "and we're moving as fast as we can. All we're getting now is bits and pieces, but there is no doubt that something's got her. She's not even really conscious at this point. She's going through the motions, but she's not talking or reacting in any usual way. It's as if we have a zombie on our hands."

"Don't even say that," Terkel ordered, yet his voice was quiet. "You have no idea how much of an effect that can have on people."

"The terminology?"

"No, the fact that there even is a zombie state," he corrected. "We don't want that to come out in public, and we certainly don't want whoever is doing this to her to be aware of the control he has over her and what that could mean in terms of what he can do."

"So, we're really thinking somebody is doing this to her?" Gage asked.

"You don't think so?" Terkel asked curiously. "I mean, you're the one who can see her. Are you saying you can't see any energy around her?"

"Not very well," he muttered, but, as they headed up the elevator, a weird staticky sound filled the air.

Terkel added, "I don't know who is doing this, but it's the same one taking out the security cameras. You'll need to check this hotel afterward and confirm no images of us are available at all," he stated.

"Which also means he's doing it remotely—or not so remotely," Gage added, turning to look up and down the hallways. "For all we know, he's in here, waiting, and picked up the signal of her presence. We also don't know whether maybe Don got a phone call at the hospital—or made one himself," he suggested. "I mean, if Don called Darren—or just spoke telepathically, for all we know—it would have alerted Darren that Sadie was at the hospital. However, what's worse is that Don could have told Darren that Sadie is potentially also an energy worker and a powerful one."

Terk noted, "I wouldn't be at all surprised if you guys have a visitor."

"*Great*," Gage muttered. "Just what we need, an attack when we're vulnerable."

"Which is the best time for an attack," Terkel stated, with a note of humor in his tone.

Morrison glared down at the phone. "Glad you find it funny."

"Not funny at all," Terk noted. "Remember that this is our life and that this is what happens. Not to mention, this is what we do," he added for emphasis, "so stay focused, and ensure nobody snatches her."

"What would they do with her if they do get her?" Morrison asked. "I mean, they can't force her to do energy work, and she's still trying to figure out what it even means to her."

"But remember, when you have somebody who can do something, it's pretty easy for them to train her and quickly. If they found any other energy workers over this time period, I wouldn't be at all surprised that they've been constantly searching for people like them because it works so well in committing these crimes."

"That would be the purpose of the beacon then," Morrison noted, groaning.

"That's what I'm thinking too," Terk confirmed. "I think the beacon is to find more lost souls, energy workers like them, so they can find that connection they seek in a group, which this crew can bring. But, at the same time, it's easy to manipulate these people into doing something because they might not even know what's happening. It's not that they aren't smart. No, it's more about they are good-hearted, don't think others have evil intents," he explained.

"That'll be the challenge with her brother, Don," Morrison suggested. "I don't know how much he even understands about what's going on, and now I'm wondering if he's really been in some fugue state himself when these robberies were happening. … I know that'll just give Sadie an unfair sense of relief, thinking that maybe it wasn't his fault, yet I don't know that that part is true."

"Again, we don't have enough information."

"Which was what was driving her crazy the whole time."

"Sure, but if she didn't see this coming, what are the chances that someone is blocking it, and if they're blocking her from getting messages or from receiving, they may have abilities to do things we are not necessarily in a position to easily fight," Terk pointed out. "So we must stand strong and ensure she gets out of this. I don't want to stop the jewelry heists only to turn around and see that she's been taken."

"God no," Morrison cried out. "We're at the hotel now."

"Get up there, lock the door, and realize that the locked door won't do anything much if they're energy workers," Terk stated. "They'll make minced meat out of that door in no time. Gage, are you there?"

"Yeah, Terk, I'm right here. I can put up somewhat of a smokescreen, but, if they're energy workers, it won't help. I can put up a bit of an energy guard too. Otherwise all I can tell you is, I've got cops on the way."

And, with that, Terkel was gone.

# CHAPTER 14

S ADIE WANTED TO talk but she couldn't say anything, as if the ability to talk had been taken from her. She struggled, realizing that she was being rushed up to the hotel room, and yet she wanted to cry out and say they were being followed, and it wasn't safe there, but she couldn't speak.

She was helpless—paralyzed—as if somebody had grabbed her vocal cords and had clamped them shut. She was functioning, in that she was on her feet and moving forward, though the men had their arms under hers and were basically dragging her down the hallway. Once in the room, she turned to stare at Morrison, her eyes wide.

She tried to reach out a hand but found that it wouldn't move. She stared down at her hands, seeing something like a spirit hand, like the spirit tied to her hand. Whatever it was called, she could lift that spirit hand out of her physical body and put it back in again. However, when she tried to move her physical body, it refused to move. Yet, when the men turned her in the direction of a chair and pushed her forward gently to sit, the momentum of their actions took her to the chair.

Morrison turned her around and gently helped her to sit down, but it wasn't an action she took on her own. It wasn't an action that she could start and complete. Yet her body carried on with its functions. How did that work? She didn't have a clue what was happening, but it was scary as she sat here, struggling, trying to figure out what to do.

She wasn't panicked, but still, she sent out a message, realizing that if anybody could help her it would be Terkel.

*I'm here*, he responded immediately. *I'm doing a scan on your system to see what's going on.*

She sagged in place, her body collapsing in on itself, as the relief worked its way through her body. She closed her eyes, grateful when that attempt to contact Terk had worked.

*You're getting a little bit more movement all the time*, he told her. *Understand that somebody else is doing this. Don't fight it, just sink into it, then toss it aside, and try to regain control of your own power based on who you are. No matter what you hear, don't let them convince you otherwise. This is a power grab. That's all it is, purely a power grab. Somebody else is trying to use your system, your body, your energy, to do what he wants.*

Her words, succinct and harsh, snapped out and filled the room, as they erupted from her in an exploded fury. "Fuck that."

Terk laughed. *Exactly, and that is exactly what you need to do*, he stated. *This person isn't used to resistance. He's not used to having anybody who can say no. So stay strong and know I'm still working on it.*

She faced Morrison, who immediately dropped down in front of her and squatted close. "Hey, glad to hear you talking."

She gave a lopsided smile. "Not quite there yet," she whispered, her voice rusty but functional. "Terkel's helping."

"Good." Morrison nodded. "I gather somebody got a hold of you."

Her eyes widened, she nodded. "Who knew?"

He gave her a ghost of a smile. "Remember what Gage said about all you would learn in just a short time?"

She nodded. "Don't like it," she muttered in a robotic tone.

"Got it," Morrison said. "Keep talking, no matter how hard it is, because, if you have control of your vocal cords, then they don't."

The thought of somebody else having control of her vocal cords was enough to make her cringe. But she jumped forward mentally and started pushing back all the shadows in her mind. As she did so, her voice got easier and easier to use, and her words started coming out smoother. Finally she could see this black ball inside her thoughts, and she quickly grabbed it and smashed it into a tighter ball, then flung it as far and as free from her soul as she could. And with that came a sense of something breaking inside, and she jumped to her feet, spun around, and almost roared with happiness. "I'm back."

She let out a loud whoop of joy and turned and grinned at them. "I don't know exactly what that was," she stated, "but I am so grateful that it's not in there anymore."

Gage walked toward her and smiled. "Congratulations. That was a very necessary step of progress in your energy work," he murmured. "You're doing great."

"What happened?"

"What happened is something that I'm sure you don't want to discuss, but you need to because, if he succeeded once, chances are he'll try again."

She nodded. "He's already trying," she confirmed in disgust, "and I have absolutely no intention of going back into that frozen fugue state again." She made a flicking motion with her hand, and then she felt a subtle change to the air. "I kicked him out of the room," she declared, as she walked over to where the food was. "If I was hungry before, you can damn-well believe I am starving now."

And, with that, both men burst into laughter. With a note of admiration, Morrison smiled at her and said, "Seems you just graduated top of the class."

"I didn't graduate from anything," she muttered, with a headshake. "I was saved, and I'm grateful to Terkel for being there to give me a hand. But if that's my brother Darren? Well, he's got another *think* coming," she declared, "because I'll never *ever* become his puppet again."

"Do you think that's what's happening to your other brother? Don seemed pretty, … well, … afraid in a way."

She nodded. "Yes, he's a puppet because he's the weaker one," she stated. "But I'm not weak, and I'm nobody's puppet, and that's just not happening. I am my own person, and Darren can go screw himself, if he thinks this relationship will be all about that."

"It could also make him very angry," Gage pointed out.

"Yeah, he's angry all right," she confirmed, "but I really don't give a damn." And she glared at him. "Right now, I need food. So, if you want to talk, we'll talk in a bit, but right now I need to eat." She stormed to the to-go bag, served herself a large portion of the food that they had brought, then sat down in front of them and ate.

THE NEXT MORNING Sadie woke early, after an incredibly hard night where she was constantly bothered by nightmares of the same thing over and over. She struggled to get to the shower, turned on the water, and stepped under the drenching heat, looking for some comfort, since she didn't get any from a good night of sleep.

By the time she was done, she felt marginally better, pushing back the nightmares a little bit more, but it was hard to experience what she had just endured. A whole realm of existence was out there that she had no idea was even possible, and now that she knew this much, it made her feel even more insecure about the world around her. There was nothing good about knowing people could do these things, and she didn't know how much of an effect it may have had on Don. Her twin brother may be under someone's thumb, and she was pretty damn sure it was Darren, the other brother, who was doing this.

So, one was dominant, one was weak, and she was an unknown factor but determined not to end up like her twin. The fact that Darren was attempting to do something along this line just pissed her off. It might just be temper on his part, but it didn't change anything as far as she was concerned. It was still not cool to stop her from doing anything. Knowing this about Darren, Sadie worried about the whereabouts of her sister, Tammy, who was still a mystery. Although, as Sadie dressed, she wondered if any updated news had been shared.

Apparently everybody was working on trying to find her sister, but Sadie was past trying to hope at this point. She would leave it in the realm of mystery for now and would try to focus on dealing with this mess with her brothers instead. Who knew what she was waking up to today?

Dressed, tired, stressed out, and wanting this whole nightmare over with, she headed out to the living room to find both Gage and Morrison sitting at the table with their laptops, working away. She stopped at the counter and grumbled, "Did you guys leave me any coffee?"

She deliberately kept her tone low and modulated, without the snap that her mood dictated. But obviously it was evident anyway. Morrison hopped up, walked over, and, without asking permission, or in any way making it look as if it was anything other than his full intention, he pulled her into his arms and gave her a gentle hug, whispering against her ear, "Sorry you had a rough night."

All her fatigue and crankiness melted away. She groaned, looked up at him. "You're way too nice." He snorted at that, even as Gage laughed out loud. She looked over at him. "And you're not nice at all."

That only served to set him off into more waves of laughter.

"You really did have a bad night, didn't you?" Morrison asked.

"Yeah, every time I turned around," she shared bitterly, "I was being attacked in a way that I didn't even know was possible. I mean, there's a whole other world out there, and nobody even knows about this." Then she stopped, frowned, and asked, "Or do they, and I'm just the dumb one who's completely in the dark?"

"Most people have no idea because most people are *not* energy workers," Gage explained. "That's the way everyone likes it really, since it keeps all that *other stuff* nicely hidden in the shadows, and nobody has to acknowledge that this energy-working stuff goes on out there. Imagine the mass panic if everybody knew."

"And yet then we could teach people how to protect themselves," she stated, staring at him. "Just like every other predator out there, we must provide at least some level of protection for people. Clearly not enough," she muttered, with a nod, acknowledging that unspoken point, "but there are at least some options for those who want to learn."

"There are opportunities for those who want to learn here too," Gage noted, looking at her steadily. "And that is something that Terkel's team, which I'm part of, … has done more than many. We are all very aware that we're extremely special in this world, and we have unique abilities to handle a certain number of problems, and the small minority of the energy workers who are bad people—like the one doing that to you—are at the root of some of the crimes in this world."

She winced. "Let's just refer to him as Darren. I'm certain it was my brother, but I've got to tell you. Right about now I'm not very interested in having a relationship with him."

"Do you—" He hesitated.

"Know for sure? Yes, it's him," she snapped. "But do I have any way to explain that to you? Definitely not."

"You don't need to," Morrison stated, a bit taken aback. "Gage and I live in a world where a lot of things go on that are hard to explain," he shared. "We trust that, if you say it's Darren, it's Darren. No evidence required."

She sagged down to the counter, even as Morrison poured her a cup of coffee and brought it over. "I'm sorry, and I guess I'll probably wind up apologizing all day." She scrubbed her face. "I thought a shower would help, but not so much. I feel as if all I did last night was wake up again and again, afraid that this guy was after me."

"This will be a hard question," Gage began, "but it's important. At any time in the night did you ever feel as if he was actually here?"

She stared at him. "Meaning they might have been real

attacks?"

"That's what I'm wondering. Did he come back, knowing your defenses were down? Or did you sense that he was coming back and kept waking up because that kept your defenses up?"

Her breath came out in a *whoosh*. "I have no idea," she replied, as if her voice was coming from afar. "This is all too new to me. And, because of that, I don't really understand the ins and outs, which just makes it that much harder to get you the answers you're looking for."

"It's not so much for my benefit, as answers you need just for your own sanity."

She winced at that. "So, it hasn't occurred to you guys yet that I might just be insane?"

Gage chuckled. "Absolutely it has," he quipped, "and we've crossed it off, even though we've met people who did cross the line into insanity through this world."

"Of course, and, if you happened to be in a group where nobody ever believes you, I just can't imagine how it would feel like to know this was all going on, and yet always doubt yourself and wonder whether it was real or not. If you guys weren't here? … Well, I just don't know what I would do."

"I think you would do just fine," Morrison replied. "You're already showing amazing depths of understanding, and, whether you believe it or not, … that is probably confounding Darren too. He may not have even known about you, then all of a sudden realizes you're here and finds himself fighting with you in a way that he hasn't had to fight before. It's probably not making him happy."

"I suspect he knows exactly who I am at this point," she stated, staring at Morrison. "I'm pretty sure Don would have told him, and, if not, well, I don't think Darren's short on skills. So I'm sure he could get that information on his own."

At that, Gage looked at her. "You want to explain that last bit?"

She shrugged. "I've just got a feeling of capability from Darren, I guess. Still some fury and frustration in his inability to do something, inability to make me do what he wanted me to do, but still, he has a lot of ability there that he probably came by through trial and error. I think he knows perfectly well who I am, and he didn't call me. He didn't talk to me in that sense, but a familiarity was there." She hesitated and then added, "The message I woke up this morning with was this. *Either you're with us or you're against us,*" she shared coolly. "I slammed a message right back at him, emphatically saying, *Against.*" She shrugged and, waving a hand around, continued. "Whether I should have or not, I don't know, but he pissed me right off."

The men smiled at her.

"That's good," Morrison noted, "because, when you get angry, you're no longer in victim mode. When you're angry, you're capable of doing all kinds of things that you didn't know you were capable of before. Unfortunately it's often things that we hadn't considered we would be dealing with. I mean, none of this is what anybody wants to deal with or things that we should even have to."

"When you sent that message back to Darren, was it a response to him talking in telepathic mode?" Gage asked.

"No. I just got this impression of words, so I fired right back," she muttered. "I know that sounds foolish, but I can't really explain it any better than that."

"It doesn't sound foolish at all," Gage stated. "I'm glad you were able to tell him that you were against it all. On the other hand, now you need to be prepared for the fact that he'll be angry, and more attacks are probably coming. As in, you're against them, and that makes you an enemy to be taken down."

Her eyes widened as she contemplated his words.

"Makes sense, doesn't it?" Morrison agreed.

"I definitely get the feeling … and it sounds strange, but Darren has so much anger inside him, so much fury that he's blended it into everything about making the world pay. I think that's what's driving all this. I don't know what's gone on in his life, and, for the first time, I would admit that I'm not sure I care in this instance. But the fact remains that Darren's scary," she declared. "He's seriously scary, and, after what he did to me already, I just want to avoid him as much as possible."

"Perfectly understandable," Morrison noted.

"If he is my brother," she added, wincing at that, "I don't know that I want a relationship with him. He has an attitude that says society owes him something, and, excuse my language, he has what I would call a fuck-the-world attitude."

At that, Gage nodded. "That's good to hear. We definitely have the same sense in this case, and, while we're not happy about whatever happened in his life, if he is trying to hold the rest of us hostage, that can't continue."

She sighed. "I know it probably won't meet with your approval, but I want to go talk to Don," she stated in a determined tone. "I think he is the weakest link, and, if anybody will talk, it's him. If anybody will give up Darren, it's Don. I don't know what kind of a grip Darren has on Don, but I can tell you that, when I'm around, the connection gets weaker. Maybe because we're twins, maybe because now I've met Darren in a sense, so I'm very much against his having anything to do with Don."

"That might be a good idea," Morrison suggested, with a look over to Gage, who nodded.

"I feel very much like a protective older sister right now," she added, with a wry look, "and even that is ludicrous, considering I've only known about Don for a few months, have barely met him. As for meeting Darren, … holy Hannah," she murmured, "that doesn't sound like fun at all."

"Then for now, just focus on protecting yourself from him," Morrison suggested.

"You two have mentioned that before," she noted, "and, while I hear you, I don't know what that looks like."

Gage nodded. "It's not as scary as it sounds. It's more about making sure he can't access your energy."

"You mean, like when he shanghaied me last night?"

"Exactly," he said, with a nod. "We have to keep that from happening again."

"Yeah, I want that too," she murmured. "There was nothing about him, or that experience, that made me want to have anything more to do with him. But, with Don, I feel differently."

"Okay then, let's go."

They soon pulled up outside the hospital. Morrison took another look at her and asked, "Are you sure?"

"I have to," she declared.

He didn't say anything more but got out, then waited for her to join him. She reached out a hand, and he smiled, instinctively holding hers. The fact that she came to him was always lovely, even if he didn't necessarily agree with what she wanted to do.

Gage hadn't argued either way, and of course the two of

them fully understood the risks involved, except Morrison wasn't sure that was really the case for Sadie. Because, at some point in time, mental health came into this, and he was certain she had never come up against something like this. Her brother Darren was causing all kinds of chaos in her world, and if speaking to Don helped her to find peace with some of this, or at least to find a way forward, then Morrison would do what he could.

As they approached the room, she looked over at him. "Do you think they'll argue with my going in?"

He shrugged. "We can certainly request that you go in, and I can pull some strings if it comes to that. Not to mention the fact that you are family, and, as long as he's allowed visitors, it should be fine."

She took a deep breath, nodded, then headed down the hallway. A guard was outside Don's room, but he only nodded as they stepped in.

"That's one thing going for us, at least." As she walked in, her brother opened his eyes, and they widened perceptibly when he saw her.

Then a smile broke out. "Hey, I wasn't sure I would ever see you again."

She walked over and picked up his hand, sitting down at his bedside. "You'll probably see me a lot more than you would like. I'm just terribly sorry for the circumstances."

"My own fault," he muttered, with a shrug.

"Maybe, but I also think Darren had a lot to do with it," she murmured. "I had a visit of sorts from him last night. So, I guess that was after you told him about me." His gaze widened instantly, and then he glanced nervously from Morrison to her and back again. She just watched and then nodded. "Yes, I know perfectly well it was Darren," she stated. "It's hard to miss that anger and that fury. I presume he didn't appreciate the fact that I came to the hospital to see you."

He winced. "I wasn't even sure I should tell him, but you're his sister too."

"Yet a sister he doesn't want in his life because I'll be that conscience he doesn't want to acknowledge. I'll be that voice he's fought against all his life," she stated. "And that is something he doesn't want."

When Don just stared at her, she nodded.

"Unlike Darren, I come from a safe, stable background, and I don't hate the world. I don't hate the people who raised me. I don't hate my other blood family members for having had a better life. I get that, from Darren's perspective, I'm somehow responsible for his bad life because I had a good life. I didn't end up killing people as a way to avenge the anger, like what is within Darren," she explained, staring at Don and not giving him the chance to pull away. "But I didn't do anything to Darren, and I will not be treated as if I had. I am not a victim, and he now knows it."

Don's breath let out in a *whoosh*, and damn if tears didn't fill his eyes again.

She leaned forward and gave him a hug.

He wrapped his arms tight around her and hung on. He didn't say anything, but his throat worked, as if he had things he wanted to say.

Morrison stayed behind her, which she was grateful for, just so her brother didn't feel quite so threatened. Morrison was big, strong, and powerful, and probably reminded Don a lot of Darren.

When Don finally released her, she settled back, a bit teary-eyed herself and added, "It's lovely to see you, and I'm so sorry for all the years we missed out on."

"Me too," he whispered. "I always knew something was missing, but I couldn't ever really explain it."

"Same for me," she agreed. "I was really angry when I found out, but my mother was dying at the time, and there wasn't any recourse other than to get as many answers as I could," she shared, with a half smile. "So, I had to come to terms with the fact that she made that decision, then chose not to tell me until she knew she was dying."

"Darren," Don said immediately.

"What about Darren?" she asked.

"He's probably the reason she didn't say anything. I think he probably knew about you, memories of you at least," he suggested, "and I think he may have approached them about us at some point. I don't know much of what happened, but I know that Darren's very angry, and I highly suspect that some of that anger is directed at you too."

"Yeah, it's definitely directed at me," she declared. As Don contemplated that, she hesitated, then looked back at Morrison, almost for permission. When he nodded, she smiled and turned back to Don. "Darren paid me a visit last night," she declared bitterly, "and it wasn't a nice one."

Her brother sucked in his breath, looking horrified. "Are you okay?" He spoke in little more than a whisper.

"I'm okay." She nodded. "But I can't say I appreciate his methods."

Don winced. "Even talking about it is so strange for me." His gaze darted to Morrison, then to her, as if he wasn't sure he should say anything.

"Don't worry about Morrison," she said, with a wave of her hand. "He sees and reads energy too."

That was almost too much for Don. "What?" he

squeaked out.

She nodded. "Of course there's always the risk we're taking even talking to you because you'll probably just tell Darren."

His gaze went from one to the other again, then he swallowed hard. In a monotone, he replied, "I'm not sure how to handle what you just said."

"The thing is, Darren thinks he's invincible, but he's not," she stated. "We're already onto him, and his visit last night just means I'll help these guys stop Darren. I was ready to ignore him, but he's dangerous," she added boldly, "particularly to me right now."

"He said he wouldn't hurt you," Don cried out. "He said he would leave you alone."

"When he stopped me from talking and from moving and tried to completely take over my system last night," she began, "I finally kicked him out. He was getting angrier and angrier the more I fought. As long as I didn't fight, he was okay, but the minute I tried to let him know that it wasn't okay, he didn't seem to handle it. So, I finally tossed him out."

Her brother just sagged back against the pillow in shock.

She nodded. "You do know you can do that too, right? Darren is not all-mighty and powerful."

Don swallowed. "I never … I never …" Then he stopped, not sure how to say it.

"You never managed to? Listen. It's probably because Darren has some way of keeping you down, maybe through the drugs for all I know. Besides, all that emotional black-mail rolling around inside is keeping you tied to him as well," she added. "I don't know the man, and obviously, after this, I'm not sure I want to, but what I have seen doesn't make me happy. Darren's not a nice person at all."

Don gave her a ghost of a smile. "Don't judge him so harshly. He's not all bad."

"He might not be all bad, but he sure hasn't shown me anything good about him," she stated, "so I'm not too anxious to help him. Not at all."

His fingers nervously pleated the sheet in front of him.

"I get that you probably don't want Morrison in here, but the fact that we don't even have cops here right now is a blessing we wouldn't have otherwise."

"Maybe," Don muttered. "I've been wondering if this room was bugged."

"I don't think so, but it's possible." She looked back at Morrison, who gave an ever-so-slight headshake. She wanted to trust him on that point. "The thing is, we can't have any more people dying because of this vendetta against the world that Darren has," she snapped. "I won't let that happen. If he hadn't come and attacked me last night, I might not have been aware of all the things he was up to—or how he'd gotten you involved in them. And, no, it certainly doesn't alleviate your guilt, but I do understand a bit more. And this is for certain. I will not play the same games."

There was fascination in Don's gaze, as if she was on to something he didn't recognize. She sighed and went on. "You really haven't had the chance to deal with many people other than Darren, have you?"

"He doesn't want me to have friends," Don shared, "and doing the kinds of stuff that I could do, I just didn't have any strength for it. He's been the one helping me."

"*Helping* you?" She snorted. "He's helping you to hurt others," she snapped, "and that's not cool." Don winced. "You've been missing that voice of conscience too."

"Sure," he agreed, his gaze hardening. "Remember that part about we didn't know you were there?"

"*You* didn't, but *he* did," she clarified, and the guilt in his expression made her wonder if he was even telling her the truth. "Of course, for all I know, he told you about me."

Don shook his head. "No, and that's another thing about Darren. He would never do that because that would be giving away a level of power he isn't prepared to give away."

"*Nice*," she muttered. "So, what will we do to stop this? Are you willing to talk to the police?"

Don shook his head. "You don't understand. Darren would kill me if I do that."

"Right, so you'll go to jail and take the blame for Darren, is that it? I mean, what does it matter that he'll get off free and clear to go steal and kill other people who had absolutely nothing to do with his rage? Darren is not an innocent bystander involved in this, while you go do hard time for the rest of your life alone." She stared at him compassionately, understanding full well that Darren's hold on Don was something he would find very difficult to get loose from.

"I'm sorry he's manipulated you so much that he has such a strong hold on you that you can't see the world around you for what it actually is."

"You mean, full of roses and puppy dogs?" he asked in a mocking tone, gaining some strength, though it was an odd strength, so unlike Don.

She studied him closely for a moment, then smiled. "Hi, Darren," she replied, with a spicy sweetness, and the shock jolted Don back. He reared up, looked at her, then blinked several times and exclaimed. "Holy crap."

"Yeah, holy crap," she murmured. "Yes, I saw him, and I recognized that it was him."

Don shook his head frantically. "He'll kill me now for sure. He'll kill me. You don't understand."

"No, I sure don't because you're not talking, and you're not helping me understand at all. What I do know is that your brother just stepped into your mind and your body, and then something changed in the way you acted."

"He's always been able to do that," Don whispered. "Ever since we were little, if somebody wanted to get into trouble, it would be me, because he'd make me confess, even though I didn't do it."

"*Hmm.*" Sadie sat back in her chair. "So you lied to me about just meeting Darren a year ago." When Don remained silent, she nodded. "Of course you'll do whatever Darren wants. It's always been that way in your life, hasn't it, Don?"

Still Don didn't reply.

"That's what Darren's hoping you'll do now too. He'll try to get you to take the fall for him, right? Why not? You've done it all your life." She turned and looked at Morrison, but the amiable look was gone from his features as he studied Don a lot more intently.

She gave Morrison a gentle smile. "Yeah, I'm learning."

"And quickly," he murmured. "I'm glad to see it."

"What is he to you?" Don asked suddenly. She was again seeing the same brother she expected to see, and she answered him. "He's a friend," she said, with a gentle smile.

"He's more than a friend."

"Not yet he isn't, but maybe in the future," she replied in complete honesty. "We have to get through this nightmare first though."

"What nightmare?" he asked suspiciously.

"You, Darren, and whoever else is in your gang," she stated. "There has to be at least one if not two more." She hesitated and then shrugged. "You came so close to talking to me, so close to trusting me, and then you backed away. I guess it's that hold Darren has over you. He's controlled you all your life, so it's pretty hard for you to recognize when you're being controlled now, isn't it?"

"I just gave up fighting," Don admitted. "It was easier to let him come and go as he wants to."

"Do you always remember what he gets you to do?"

"No, sometimes I blank out if it's ugly."

She sat back and shuddered under the weight of the understanding. "You don't even realize when somebody is dying, do you? When he's shooting people?"

"I'm not looking," he muttered.

"That's because you know how wrong it is, how horrible what you're doing to other people is, and yet you're okay with him using you."

"No, I'm not okay with it or with him. I just blank out in order to make it go away," he cried out in frustration. "You don't understand what it's like to have him around."

"Okay, so tell me this. ... What if he's *not* around?"

"My brother is many, many things, but he is not as easy to get rid of as you think."

"No, I'm not at all surprised," she murmured, and, with that, she stood up. "I came to see you, to see if there was any way to talk sense into you, but I can see that you don't really want to have anything to do with me."

"I absolutely do want to have something to do with you," he cried out. "However, I can't deal with him at the same time."

She nodded. "I'll come back later and talk to you."

"Okay. Do you promise?" Such a pathetic, plaintive tone filled his voice that she walked over and hugged him again.

"I promise," she whispered.

And, with that, she headed out to the door and to Morrison. Outside the doorway, with the guard looking at her, she stepped a few feet away, looked down at her trembling hands, then looked back up at Morrison and whispered, "What the hell was that?"

MORRISON LED SADIE out of the hospital and into the vehicle, where he stood outside and contacted Terkel.

Terk greeted him by saying, "Something very strange is going on."

"I'm definitely getting strange vibes," Morrison agreed, looking at her shaking hands.

"We need to get her back home and keep her safe. She's very susceptible to whatever this is," Terkel murmured. "Just so you know, Don is doing fine medically speaking, and he's being moved to the local jail today. As a matter of fact, that transfer should be happening very soon."

"Okay, I'll tell her that," Morrison said. "I'll take her back home again and see if I can help her to decompress."

"We have the address for the other brother," Terkel added, "so we're sending somebody over there to see if we can pick him up."

"It would be great if you could, though I don't know what we're supposed to do to stop him from whatever else he is capable of doing."

"That's a whole different challenge," Terkel agreed, with a snort. "As you know, this stuff always freaks people out."

"Sure, and what are we supposed to do in the meantime?" Morrison asked.

"Stay calm, stay safe, and keep, … well, try to keep Sadie balanced and aware another attack could happen at any time."

"Got it," he murmured. He got back into the driver's side and shared, "Terkel says a team is heading to pick up Darren at his home."

She looked at him in surprise. "They found an address for him?"

He nodded. "Apparently so, and they're on their way."

"Perfect," she murmured.

"It might help us if he's distracted by them, so we're heading home, and you're supposed to stay calm, cool, and collected, knowing they are on it."

"*Great*," she muttered. "In other words, try not to think about all the craziness going on."

"Exactly," he murmured.

Once back at the hotel, he kept a wary eye on Sadie. Morrison wasn't sure just what had gone on in the hospital, having picked up on something that made absolutely no sense. Still, he wasn't sure about even talking to her about it. She had enough to deal with right now as it was and had done incredibly well, considering her lack of training and experience in this, Yet what he was hearing, seeing, and thinking was a step even beyond that.

Back in the hotel room, he smiled at her and asked, "Coffee?"

"Sure," she murmured. "We should have picked it up."

"We should have. I was thinking we would go back to your place, but …"

"Maybe I can now."

"No, you can't, not yet," he stated, "but, hey, these are the facts of life right now." He pondered his options and quickly texted Gage. "Gage is on his way back, so he'll pick up coffee and some more food."

She smiled. "He does well as a delivery boy, doesn't he?"

"I suspect he's great at whatever he does and happily does whatever is needed to be done," he shared, with a smile. "It really is a case of day to day. We don't worry about the little things as far as roles and who does what. We just get it done. There are plenty of other things to worry about right now."

She nodded. "I won't argue with that either," she whispered. "I just want to know that everything will be okay."

Inside the room she paced nervously, making him wonder if this really was the best location for her.

"What about taking a trip back to my apartment?" she suggested. "At least there I could potentially grab some fresh clothes."

He pondered that and then shrugged. "That may be something we can make work."

"Yes, I could really use some clothes."

"Yeah, I'll talk to Gage about it when he gets here." She smiled and settled down immediately, playing games on her phone for something to do. When Gage walked in with coffee a little bit later, Morrison presented her request. Gage pondered it and then shrugged.

"If we make it fast, then sure, why not?" Gage sent off a message to Terkel to let him know what they had planned. As soon as the coffee was gone and the sandwiches Gage had brought were consumed, he led the way back outside.

They hopped into Gage's vehicle this time and headed over to her apartment.

"It feels so strange to even think about going back there, and yet it's my home."

"It is your home, but now everything feels different," Morrison stated. She didn't say anything to that, but, as they approached, he felt her getting more and more nervous. They walked up to her apartment, grateful that absolutely nothing was untoward. As she quickly packed up a bag of personal belongings and started to step outside, his phone rang.

He answered it and froze, grabbing her by the arm and pulling her back inside. With Gage standing there, staring at him, clearly worried, Morrison quickly ended the call, looking at her with a concerned expression. "Don escaped while being moved from the hospital to the corrections facility," he shared. "And it was hours ago."

She stared up at him, a smile breaking free, and then she immediately realized the ramifications and sighed. "I'm not supposed to be happy about that, am I?" She shook her head. "I'm so confused over the whole thing. I don't know how much is him and how much is our brother."

"Exactly," Morrison agreed, "so, for the moment, try not to be too happy about it."

"But it's not as if he'll come here," she stated. Then she pondered that. "He won't really. No, I don't think so, but I'm not sure where he's going and why."

"You did startle him at the hospital with your knowledge of his crew, along with your energy skills."

"I know," she muttered, as she glanced around. "I've had a really strange feeling for the last little while."

"You and me both," Gage announced. She looked at him, and he nodded. "Definitely an odd feeling, I just don't know what it is."

"No, I don't know either," she admitted, "but it's as if we're being watched, but not being watched."

Morrison interjected, "Because we're being watched on the ethers."

As she stiffened, Gage nodded.

"That's it." Gage gave Morrison a slug to his shoulder. "That's exactly it. Somebody is tracking us, not in person, but out there."

Morrison nodded. "That's my take on it." He looked around, then announced, "It really won't matter where we are, but ..." He looked back at Gage. "I'm not getting the sense of them planning on coming here, but I can't trust that, as I'm not really getting the sense of anything at this point."

Gage frowned and nodded. "Let me see if I can get some help tracking this," he murmured, as he stepped a few feet away and contacted Terkel. When he got off the phone, his voice was deep and dark as he added, "One of the policemen was badly injured in the escape."

"Crap," she whispered. "That won't go well for Don."

"None of it was supposed to go well for him anyway," he murmured to her. "Remember that. We already have a dead security guard and innocent bystanders have been killed left, right, and center on the other heists, so nobody will go easy on Don anyway. No way that's happening."

Morrison nodded. "Which is why he's on the run because he believes there is no other option."

Sadie asked, "Is there any chance, ... any chance it will go easier on Don if it wasn't him but Darren controlling him?"

"How will you prove it?" Gage asked.

She winced and shook her head. "Nobody'll believe it, will they?"

"No, they won't," he stated. "That's always one of the challenges that we face when we do this energy work. Those who can get away with it, get away with it, and those who can't get away with it will pay the price."

She swallowed and nodded. "I feel as if we need to move." She suddenly headed for the front door. As soon as she got there and reached for the knob, it opened, and Don stepped in. She looked at him and smiled. Then her smile fell away. "As much as I'm happy to see you, I really wish you hadn't escaped."

He just nodded, then looked at her, over at Morrison, and his frown settled into something much deeper and uglier. Then he turned to face Gage. "Wow, you really do have protectors here, don't you?"

Morrison studied him, not sure exactly what he was seeing. Again not liking anything about this, he reached into Don's energy. He could tell from Gage that he was correct, and something was very off. But before he had a chance to say anything, Don raised his hand to reveal a handgun and pointed it directly at Gage.

"I don't like anything about you," he said with a snarl.

Then she stepped right in front of the gun and looked at him in shock. "What are you doing?" she cried out. "He's done nothing but help me."

He glared at her. "Help you do what?" he asked. "Help you to get us? Help turn you against your family? What help is that?"

"I'm not turning against you at all," she cried out.

But he wouldn't hear any of it. Of course, from his perspective, she'd done nothing but turn against him. Just as Morrison went to say something, the gun turned in his direction, and that same hard voice echoed again.

"Don't speak."

# CHAPTER 15

S HOCKED, SADIE TURNED and looked back at Don. "What are you doing?" she wailed.

He motioned at her. "Walk to the door."

Numb, she looked at the other two men, sensing that they were both tensing, ready to jump. She shook her head at them. "Please, don't get shot."

"Not as if we'll have much choice," Gage noted, his tone hard.

She closed her eyes, then turned to her brother. "I'll go with you, but you can't shoot them." He glared. "That's the only condition I have," she stated.

"You do realize I have the gun," he stated, "which means that I get to call the shots."

She stuck her chin out pugnaciously. "Not if you expect to have me not cause trouble the whole way," she muttered. "I'll go with you willingly and peaceably, but you don't get to shoot them."

"Fine," he muttered, pointing at the door. "But, if they leave this property any time within the next hour, I will shoot them the next time I see them. Do you hear me?"

She turned and looked at the others. Morrison snapped, "No promises."

Don laughed. "Just means I'll shoot you the next time I see you." As soon as she was out the door, he pointed it back at them. "Now I really want to just pop you right now."

But Sadie grabbed his arm and pulled him out. "You promised."

"I did not," he snapped. "I did not promise, and I wouldn't promise. These guys are trying to put me in jail."

"No, they're trying to stop you from killing people," she said in exasperation, "and now I can see that it's obviously for good reason."

He turned the gun on her, and she just stared up at him. "Is that what it is now?" she asked. "You finally get to meet your twin sister that you didn't know you had, and you're ready to kill her?" she asked, tears coming to her eyes. She wiped them away impatiently. "Then just shoot me now," she spat. "Don't worry about shooting them, just shoot me."

"Don't—"

"I don't really give a crap," she cried out, tears already threatening to choke her. And it was true. At that moment, she didn't give a crap. She didn't want to die by any means. She didn't want anything to do with death, but neither could she sit here and watch Don shoot down the people who had done so much for her. "I can't believe that's who you are, Don."

"It's because you don't want to see anything," he muttered, "especially my brother."

"Isn't he the one making you do this?" she asked, looking at him.

"He's at home," he said, with a shrug. "I'm taking you over there now."

She looked up at him. "Then don't shoot them. They don't know where he lives, so just let them go. I'll go with you."

He hesitated, then looked back at the others. Both had

their hands up. "I mean it, if I see you again, you know what will happen."

They both just nodded.

And, with that, he slammed the door shut, then, grabbing her hand, ran through the hallway, then down the stairway. Once they were outside, he shoved her into a van, then started laughing, almost hysterically. "Now that was fun," he declared, with a grin.

She wasn't even sure what to think because how could he find something like that entertaining when he'd obviously terrorized so many people? She sank back into her seat, staring at him.

He laughed. "You know, with you being able to do energy, we will be invincible."

"To do what?" she asked. "Go shoot and kill more people?"

"If they behave, we won't have to shoot them." He laughed and added, "Anyway, you can talk to Don anytime you want to now."

And just like that, he shifted, and she looked at him in shock. "How can you let him take you over like that?" she asked Don, remembering the personality change when he almost shot Morrison.

Don shuddered. "I'm sorry. He's always been able to do that."

She sagged into her seat, wondering how to get him to stop giving over control to Darren.

"And, besides," he added in a defensive tone, "I can't just stop him from popping in. He's very strong."

She groaned. "I gather we'll go see him now."

"Yes, that's what he wants me to do." He looked at her and smiled. "That'll be the first time we've gotten the family together in all this time. Except for your sister."

"Our sister," she corrected.

"I know, but I don't even know anything about her." Don chewed on a fingernail, even as he drove. "Maybe Darren can sort it out."

Sadie rolled her eyes, not at all sure that Darren could do anything at this point. He seemed to be nothing but a big bully. As they drove, she kept trying to send messages out mentally, until finally Don looked at her. "They can't hear you. You know that, right?"

"Why can't they hear me?" she asked.

He shrugged. "We always block everything around us so they can't."

She didn't know what to say to that and sat silently as the miles rolled by, until he finally pulled into an apartment complex. She frowned because it looked familiar. She cast a sideways glance at Don. "How long have you been connected with him?" she murmured.

"Forever," he said in a passionate tone. "He's always been there. He's always looked after me."

"That's not what you told me before. You said you met him at the pool hall or something just a year ago."

"I didn't even know you. It's not as if I'll tell you all about us."

"Of course, that loyalty, that family bond, ... that's what I didn't get."

"Nope, but you got a lot of other things."

She winced at that because his voice kept shifting. She nodded, wanting to tell the other brother to take a hike and disappear, but she didn't know what would happen if she even started that. And it probably wasn't the most sensible thing to do when she was sitting here in a vehicle with somebody who was obviously intent on using the gun in his hand. She was grateful that he hadn't shot Morrison or Gage. "Thank you for not killing them," she whispered.

He looked at her, hesitated, then nodded. "Obviously you care about that one, but it's really shitty that you would go hook up with a cop."

"He's not really a cop," she clarified. "He's been in Special Forces, and now I don't know exactly what he is."

He laughed. "So, he doesn't even have a job. That's rich."

"Oh, he has a job, but it's not one that he can really talk about."

She hadn't at any point in time even questioned Morrison about it. It's not as if there'd been time to discuss such things or to even contemplate that there would even be such an issue going forward. Regardless she just wanted to see him after this. That wasn't something that she had thought about either, until her brother had brought it up.

"How serious is it?" Don asked.

"We haven't had a chance to be serious at all," she murmured.

He grimaced. "It doesn't seem you'll get that chance either." He shrugged. "Our brother isn't exactly the easiest person to get along with." And, with that, he smiled at her. "So, come on. Let's go meet him," he said, his voice suddenly boyish. "You'll like him."

"How can you even say those two sentences back-to-back and expect me to like Darren?" she murmured to herself, since Don was already out of the vehicle, waiting for her, the gun nowhere in sight. Relieved at that, she headed with him up to the apartment building. As she got closer, she realized it was the same place where they had found him.

"How are you feeling, by the way?" she asked cautiously.

"I'm fine. Sometimes I get a bad trip, and that's unfortunate, but, hey, I can't really blame anybody but myself for it."

"I'm sorry the drugs have such a strong hold on you," she murmured.

He looked at her and asked her curiously, "You haven't done drugs?"

She shook her head.

"That's all right," he replied, with an excited laugh, "you'll like it."

She stiffened at that. "I don't want anything to do with drugs," she declared.

"Once you've been with us for a while, you will," he stated. "We all do drugs. It's a great way to unwind."

Not liking anything about the direction they were going, she carefully walked at his side, looking around.

"They're not coming after you," Don said. "I sent an energy blast, something you probably don't know how to do yet." He laughed. "From what I gather, it would have hit them pretty hard."

She froze in place and turned to look at him. "You said you wouldn't hurt them."

"No, I didn't," he clarified, looking at her. "I said I wouldn't shoot them."

She swallowed hard. "How badly are they hurt?"

"No idea. I've never been around to see the repercussions afterward." Don shrugged. "For all I know, it's not even much of a blast."

"Yet you're expecting it to be devastating."

"I'm expecting it to at least give us a head start."

"And yet you came back here, why?"

He looked around and frowned. "Yeah, that probably wasn't the smartest move, was it?"

He hesitated, and she realized her mistake. "But, if your brother is here, I'm sure it'll be okay."

He looked at her, then back at his apartment and nodded. "Yeah." Yet confusion filled his tone, as if he wasn't sure what was going on.

She definitely wasn't at all sure what was going on. Something strange was happening, and she didn't know how to get to the bottom of it.

She was desperately trying to stop Don from doing anything that would hurt his chances of ever getting out of prison, but, for all she knew, it was already well past that point from the jewelry heists and people killed, plus he hurt a cop in his escape. He didn't kill him at least. "You didn't hurt that cop too badly, did you?" she whispered.

He looked at her, then shook his head, looking confused. "No, no, of course not," he said, clearly puzzled. "I didn't hurt any cop."

That explained all of it. His brother Darren had been in control at that point in time. As they headed to the stairs, she tried to stay with him, but he was moving at a rapid rate. "Hang on," she cried out. "Apparently you aren't hurt at all because, man, you are moving."

"I always move at a good clip, even with a supposedly weak heart," he said, laughing. "What's with you?" he jeered. "You should be in much better shape than this." It was a side of her brother that she didn't know, having not had any experience or contact with him outside of the hospital. But it was also a part of him that she wasn't sure she liked either.

Maybe only now, after the first wave of joy that she had brothers had passed, was she realizing just how protective and sheltered her upbringing had been. As they got up to the apartment, the same one where she had first found Don, she asked, "I thought we were going to your brother's apartment?"

He looked at her, surprised, then nodded. "We are."

At that she slowly closed her mouth, not sure what was happening as they walked up to the very same apartment where Don had been found. She thought it had been his apartment, but maybe it had been rented under his brother's name. Sighing at that, she walked in, expecting to see Darren here. As she searched the area, she turned back and looked at him. "He's not here."

Don looked around, frowned, picked up his phone, and started calling. "He should be," he snapped. "He should be right here."

She just nodded and waited. Not exactly sure what had gone wrong, all she knew was that, from the perspective of her brother Don, something was very, very wrong.

MORRISON SLOWLY PICKED himself up off the floor. The blast had come out of nowhere, and he'd been hard-pressed to even protect himself, as if shot off his feet and onto the floor. Gage had caught a similar blow, but now they were both sitting up and looking around at the room and at each other. "And yet he hadn't pulled this at the jewelry stores, correct?"

"I don't know," Gage admitted. "We don't have any camera footage."

"Right."

"I'm wondering if that's really how he managed to stop

everything from working electronically."

"It's possible," Morrison noted.

They both got up, and Gage was checking himself out. "I'm not seriously hurt, so I'll take that as a good thing."

"Me too, but she's gone, and that sucks," Morrison muttered, as he looked around. "Where the hell is he taking her?"

Gage nodded. "To his brother's apartment."

"We already set a team there, right?" At that, he grabbed his phone and put it on Speaker, as Terkel answered. "Terkel, Don came and took her away," Morrison stated, not in any way minimizing the damage they had been through. "We couldn't stop him. He had a gun and got her cooperation by threatening to shoot us, then used an energy blast as they left, that knocked us off our feet for a bit," he shared. "We're both fine, but I don't know what the hell that was."

"No, I don't know either," Terkel replied. "We have more dark news for you."

"What's that?"

"We're not sure exactly what's going on here, but the team went to the brother's apartment."

"Right, any chance you guys picked up Darren?" he asked hopefully.

"Not only did we not pick him up but … he's dead."

"What do you mean, he's dead?"

"He's dead and had been for at least six hours, if not longer."

Morrison turned and looked at Gage in shock. "How is that even possible? How long ago did Don escape custody?" Morrison asked Terk.

"About six or so hours ago," Terkel replied. "So, whatever is going on, … it involves Don, but I don't know who else."

"Is there any chance it doesn't involve anybody else?" Morrison asked, still working on that theory he had from that last visit to the hospital.

"I mean, it's possible, but everything we've heard so far indicated four involved in the heists, three inside, and a driver, we presumed."

"What if it was just the two of them? Just Don and Darren? Did the cops find the jewels?"

"No, not yet," Terk said. "They're tearing apart Darren's place. They've just moved the body out," he added.

"But she's supposed to be on her way there. Or … Don's gone back to his place."

"Why would he do that? I mean, he almost died there."

"And yet we don't know how he got the drugs, or even if they were self-administered," Morrison reminded Terk. "What are the chances that Don killed his brother as soon as he escaped, then came to get Sadie, all before we ever found Darren, as a way to stop him?"

It made sense, and what was starting to make sense also scared the scrap out of Morrison. He and Gage raced toward the one address that they knew, and that was the apartment where they had found Don in medical distress. Whatever happened to Don all happened in this one area, and they needed to get there before something else terrible happened.

Morrison didn't know whether Don had a suicide pact going on or maybe wanted to wipe out his family, then disappear. Yet Morrison knew that Sadie might think she was safe because she and Don were family, twins even, but Morrison thought that naïveté might put her in even more jeopardy.

# CHAPTER 16

S ADIE STOOD IN the center of the living room. "Now what?"

Don frowned as he wandered through the apartment. "He told me that he would be here," he said, looking back at her, "so he must be on his way."

She nodded and didn't say anything, not sure that she was looking forward to meeting Darren as it was. Everything she had learned about him so far didn't exactly endear her to him. After ten minutes of Don just pacing, she finally intervened. "Do you want to text him and ask where he is?"

He looked at her, startled, then pulled out his phone, checked for any messages, and shrugged. "He doesn't like it if I bug him."

Her breath came out with a *whoosh*. "I guess you don't do anything that upsets him, *huh*?"

"No, I don't. It's generally not worth it."

She snorted. "And that," she whispered, "is the problem."

"No matter what you say to me, he's still my brother," he stated, and he flashed her a hard look. "And yours too."

"I get that, but did you ever wonder if something was wrong in our family?"

"Like maybe something is seriously wrong with all of us?" He glared at her. "I'm not listening to that talk," he muttered. "Besides, if there is, it's too damn bad. The world didn't treat us nice, and there's nothing we can do about it."

"And yet," she replied, looking at him. "there is quite a lot we *could* do about it."

He immediately shook his head again. "Time to stop talking," he said in a less-than-cheerful tone.

She immediately shut up but stared at him because he was so mercurial. His moods shifted from one to the other, and she didn't have any warning as to when he would flip. It made him uncomfortable to be around.

All the times she was thinking about having contact with her brother, it never once occurred to her that she would be in danger or that he would ever try to hurt her. Why? She just wanted to get to know him. And, if he didn't want that, theoretically that would be okay too. But *this*, whatever it was, scared her. She sat here very quietly, contemplating her options, when Don suddenly flopped himself down on the couch across from her.

"He should be here soon."

She just nodded and didn't say anything.

"You don't believe me, do you?" he snapped.

She looked at him cautiously. "It's not that I don't believe you," she clarified. "I've just never really met him, so I don't know him at all. I don't know what he's like."

"He's mean," he said suddenly. "He's chaotic, and he's often out of control."

She winced. "You're not making me want to get to know him either."

He snorted. "As if you think you'll get an option? He's family, and you do right by family."

"And if you don't do right by family?"

"Then you take family out."

He said it with such certainty that her heart froze. And right then and there, for the first time, she realized that she could be looking at some serious mental illness in the family. She swallowed. "You didn't do that though, did you?"

He looked at her. "Do what?"

"You were talking about taking family out."

"No, I didn't," he argued, his tone scruffy. "You were asking what to do with family that's no good, weren't you? You take them out because what else will you do?"

"Why?"

"You can't deal with them. They're batshit crazy at times," he said, with a shrug. "So, what's the option?"

She just nodded and watched.

He smiled. "You're afraid I'll take you out, aren't you?" he asked, with sudden insight.

"It certainly occurred me," she muttered. "I mean, it's not as if you're giving me any reason to doubt it."

"Maybe, yet you don't have any reason to doubt me."

She wasn't so sure about that. "I'm glad that you're feeling better. The hospital must have been hard on you."

"Yeah, I'm feeling better, and the cops didn't really give me much of a fight. But then again, it's not as if they ever do."

"Because you used energy on them?"

"Yeah," he said, looking at her. "It's pretty easy really, but I wasn't sure how it would work in a courthouse with a lot of people around. If I could get judged by a jury alone, then maybe, but, with everybody there, it's really hard," he admitted. "And I'm not all that good with it anyway, which is why Darren used to get so mad at me."

"I'm sorry he got mad at you. As much as you love your brother, I'm sure he's not been easy to deal with."

"He's not *my* brother. He's *our* brother," he stated, glaring at her.

"Sorry, it's just such a new thing to even understand for me. Pardon me for messing it up all the time." She felt as if she was walking on eggshells around Don, and he was so different now from the frightened boy she had met in the hospital that she didn't know what to say. "Did you go to school?"

"Sure, I went to school. It's not as if you have a choice. I went for a while, at least."

"But you didn't graduate?"

He looked at her, and his eyebrows shot up. "No, I got into gangs, and my brother got me out of gangs," he stated. "So, that was one good thing Darren did for me."

"That is a good thing," she agreed immediately. "I've heard they can be pretty hard on the people trying to get out."

"That's true. I think Darren killed one of them." Don stated it in such a matter-of-fact and informative way that it took her breath back.

"Oh," she replied in a small voice.

He looked up and laughed. "You see? Our worlds are just so different. To me, that's not even hardly worth mentioning, but, to you, it's the shock of a lifetime."

"And yet it shouldn't be," she noted, with a small smile in his direction. "After all, you guys killed what, four people in the heists by now?"

He looked at her, then pondered it for a moment and replied in a casual tone, "Yeah, I think so."

"And you have no remorse over it?"

"It's not as if I wanted to or if I enjoyed it," he clarified. "I guess they were just not supposed to go to work that day."

"Oh, so just like that, they're not supposed to go to work, and, if they did, well, you guys are justified to kill them?"

He just looked at her as if she were being obtuse, and, to a certain extent, she was. She just didn't get it.

She didn't understand what was going on here. She shifted on the couch, getting a little more comfortable and yet still felt edgy, still wondering if she should make a dash for the door. And yet she wasn't sure what he would do if she did, or what she would do, depending on his reaction. Would she fight him? And, if that gun came back out again, then what?

The thought of being in a gunfight with the twin brother she had spent months trying to get close to, imagining that dream life of building a great relationship with him, well, … it was looking mighty foolish right now. "I guess I was really naïve, wasn't I?" she murmured.

He looked at her. "I don't know, were you? What does that even mean?"

"It's just that I didn't understand. I didn't understand what your life was like."

"How would you? It's not as if you ever had the chance to see our life, so how would you know?"

Again, that same calm matter-of-fact demeanor. "When did you get into drugs?" she asked him.

"Decades ago," he said, with a laugh, and then he shrugged. "So, maybe not decades but definitely a long time ago," he clarified. "It was just the light stuff for a while, but it very quickly gets a hold of you, and then you go downhill after that. Once you're into drugs, and you don't have a regular job, then you've got to keep feeding the habit, and that means you head into a life of crime." He stared off in the distance, as if looking back over his life. "And it's pretty hard, once you're into the criminal crap, to ever get out again."

"Yet you got out of the gangs."

"I did," he confirmed, looking at her. "But again that took help from my brother." Then he stopped, looked at her, and smiled. "*Our* brother was already a criminal."

She laughed. "No, you're right, *our* brother," she said, with a nod.

"You shouldn't forget it, you know? It'll upset him if you do."

"Ah, well, I'm not trying to. The last thing I want to do is upset him."

"No, but see, trying not to, even if you keep trying, doesn't mean that you get off with it," he explained. "If you have to keep trying, it means it's not a priority. It means he's not a priority. I'm just telling you that he won't like it if you continue to not make him a priority."

"Okay," she said agreeably, still unsure how to handle Don's moods. His upbringing had been so different from what she'd been through that none of it made any sense to her, and yet it wasn't Don's fault. So, how could she blame him for it? And it's not that she wanted to blame anybody, but she really, really wanted this whole scenario to go away.

When his phone rang, he looked down at it and shut it off.

"Not anybody you want to talk to?" she asked.

"No, sure not," he said, as he glared at the door.

"How long do we wait?"

He replied, "As long as it takes."

"Okay." She wasn't sure what to say to that either. She settled in for a longer wait, considering that they'd already been here for a while. "Do you have any coffee?"

He shook his head. "No, I don't drink coffee."

"I would really like a cup."

"Too bad. I don't have any."

"Okay. Do you have any games you want to play?"

He stared at her.

"We're just sitting here, and you don't want to talk, but I don't want to sit here and do nothing. It'll just help the time go by."

"Where did you go to school?" he asked suddenly.

She named the place, and he nodded. "Did you go to high school?"

"I did, and I went to college," she added.

"Of course you did," he muttered, with an eye roll for emphasis. "But I've still probably made more money than you have."

"Possibly. I gave up making money in order to look after Mom."

"She wasn't *Mom*," he yelled, almost spitting with rage. "Mom's dead."

Sadie sucked in her breath, once again stunned at the shock and the transformation in his moods, and nodded, realizing he was easily triggered. "She is," she agreed, "and, for that, I'm very sorry. I would have loved to have known her."

He seemed to calm down at that again, and finally, when she couldn't take it anymore, she had to ask him, "What are you waiting for?"

He looked at her. "Can't you feel the energy?"

"Where?"

"Somebody's coming," he said, with a bright smile.

"No, I can't feel anything," she admitted, looking

around, wondering. "I thought you had something to stop people from finding you."

"I do, but I dropped it so Darren can come in. Now I can feel him coming."

"Ah, okay," she said, as she settled back to wait, staring at the door. When nobody was here after another five minutes, she looked over at Don, but he was puzzled too, staring at the door.

She opened her mouth to say something, but he immediately lifted his hand to stop her. She snapped her mouth shut and sent out a warning to anybody who might be coming. Almost as soon as she did that, the door burst open, and Morrison stepped inside.

AT THE SIGHT of him, Don snapped to his feet, racing for the gun that he'd put down somewhere. Morrison caught him by the back of his neck and tossed him to the floor, then quickly landed on his back and secured his arms behind him with handcuffs.

She stared down at Don and told Morrison, "I don't know what's going on."

"I know, but hopefully it's about to end right now." He picked Don up, and she watched as two cops and Gage stepped inside.

She walked over to Gage. "What's going on?"

"How's he been?" Gage asked, with a head nod to Don.

"Erratic."

He nodded. "That's probably a good word for it."

"You want to explain?" She looked back at her brother, who was glaring at her solemnly.

Gage asked, "What happened? What are you doing here? Who are you waiting for?"

"Darren. We've been sitting here waiting for him to arrive."

Gage looked back at Don. "You want to tell her, or should I?"

Her brother stared at Gage in surprise. "Tell her what?"

"You need to tell her what you did."

"I didn't do anything," he said in a small voice.

She looked back at Gage. "I don't understand. What's going on?"

He sighed. "We went to Darren's place to pick him up."

"Oh, good," she muttered, relief washing over her.

Gage studied the relief on her face and then shook his head. "No, not quite so good."

She frowned.

"He's dead. And this guy killed him."

"I didn't. I didn't. I didn't," Don cried out. "I didn't. I didn't kill him." He stared around the room in a panic. "No. We were supposed to kill each other, and it was supposed to be all of us going out at one time because we knew that the police would get us at some point." He was frantic and sounded like a broken radio. "So we were supposed to die, but not until he got her." Then he stopped. "I don't think Darren would really go through with it though."

"You don't think he wanted to go through with it, or *you* weren't going through with it?" she asked intently.

"I don't think Darren wanted to go through with it, and I had to ensure he did."

"Why is that?" she asked.

And then Don started to cry. "So, I could finally be free of him."

Morrison watched as the sympathy crossed Sadie's face, but he held up a hand. "Oh no you don't, not yet," he told Sadie, before turning his gaze on her brother. "That's a good story, Don, but there's another part to this, isn't there?" At that, Don turned to him. Then Don's face twisted and out snapped the other voice she had heard before.

"I don't give a shit what that little piss-ass says," the new voice spat. "Darren deserved to die. He treated us like shit since day one, ever since he found us. I couldn't wait to get a chance to pay him back. You better believe I killed him," And then he smiled, looking from one to the other, and Don's face had completely morphed into someone else's. He looked over at Sadie. "Hey, sis. I guess you don't know me, *huh?*"

She got up and walked closer. "For a while there I was afraid it was Darren."

"No, Darren is just as weak as Don is. I'm the strong one. I'm the one who runs this ruse," he declared. "Don just does what I say, and Darren did too."

"Who are you?" she asked.

"They call me Bob, Bob the builder. We split personalities many, many years ago—after one of our foster homes treated us really badly, and Don couldn't handle it. He went inside, and, as soon as he did, I popped up and took over. I let him out every once in a while because that was healthy for him, and I want to keep him safe."

"What about Darren?" she asked.

"Darren, well, he wasn't as weak as his brother Don, so that's why I had to kill him," Bob shared. "I mean, there can't be two bosses, and he was getting worried about the way things were getting a little more erratic with Don, and I had been a little harder to control. Plus, the more energy work we did, the more Don was coming into his own. I just can't have that, no way. I'm the boss, nobody else."

She stared at him, as if finally realizing what was going on. "Couldn't you just let Don have a life?"

"No, I can't. He doesn't want a life. He just wants to be taken care of now. He's had enough of what people can do to him," he stated, staring at her. "Not everybody got to have the nice, sweet little life that you had." He watched her for a moment and added, "See? You're already ready to bawl." He gave her a mock shudder. "I'll never be that weak again." He shook his head. "We were weak once, but not anymore, not again. Nobody'll ever hurt us like they did back then."

"I'm sorry," she whispered. "Even though it was a long time ago, I'm sorry for what you went through."

He laughed. "Don't be because that made us strong, and it made us realize what we could do. But Darren started to understand the energy stuff. Once he realized that we could all do it, I think he thought he could help Don get free of me."

"So, Darren had to go."

He gave a hard laugh. "Nobody gets free of me."

She sucked in her breath. "And the suicide pact?"

"Don really does want to commit suicide," he noted, "but I couldn't let him do it, although I was more than happy to have Darren dead and gone, which was no skin off my teeth. The man was a loose cannon."

"So, you're the one who killed all those people, right? But why go do all the jewelry heists if you were just committing suicide anyway?"

"I wasn't going to. We were just using the suicide as a ploy to get rid of Darren that way, and it worked," he declared. "Now we have lots of money and don't have to worry about it anymore, but, if we do, we'll just do another heist. We weren't going to do any more, after that last one went sideways with too much bloodshed," he shared, with a shudder. "I really don't like all that blood, but it's a necessary part of this."

"It's not necessary at all," she stated. "You could easily have robbed those stores without killing people."

"It's hurt or get hurt," he snapped. "You really haven't learned anything, have you?"

"Apparently not," she noted. "At least not anything that matters to you."

"That's true." He snorted, then looked over at Morrison and Gage. "Once I realized these guys were energy workers, and I could feel that power in them, I knew that the game was up. I probably should have let Darren kill Don, since prison won't be much fun."

"I don't know that you'll get to prison either," she stated. "You probably won't be considered fit to stand trial. They will lock you up in a little padded cell and leave you there." He glared at her, and she shrugged. "Just listen to you right now. Split personalities are not well assimilated into a general population," she pointed out.

"Not our fault, it's those assholes who abused us," Bob declared, his voice hardening. "Even Darren had a shitty life, but, hey, he was trying to take me out of the picture, so it's our life now."

She just nodded, not knowing what else to say. When the two cops each reached for an arm on either side, he stopped, shifted personalities, then asked her, "Will you come visit me?" The plea was in Don's plaintive voice.

She smiled at him. "Of course I will," she replied, and, with that, he was led outside. She walked over to Morrison and collapsed against his chest. He wrapped his arms around her and held on tight.

"Are you okay?" he asked.

"I am. It's just shitty the way the whole thing worked out. I was so hoping to have some family."

He nodded. "And yet it won't be an easy time. Not once we realized what they were involved in. They each had an ugly side."

"And the drugs, … apparently Don's been heavily into drugs for a very long time," she added.

"Yeah, and that can have a huge effect on people too," Morrison agreed. "Darren also left information on the other two hired hands involved in the heists. They are being picked up now. Penny is one, down as their driver, which won't make you happy. However, Don is not the father to Penny's son. So he's not your nephew. The kid just had contact with his mom who had contact with Don, as the driver on these heists."

"This story just keeps getting sadder."

"Yeah, well, the fourth member of their crew was a part-time security guard at one of the jewelry stores."

She looked up at him and groaned.

"But," Morrison added, "we now have Don's gun. This may be the evidence needed to get a conviction—or a psych ward stay."

Sadie sighed. "Can I go back to my place now, please? I just want to forget about all this."

"Absolutely," he agreed, as he looked over at the cops, who were still talking in the hallway. "You'll have to give a statement."

She winced. "That'll be fun."

"I know. It'll be hard, but this way you can be completely honest."

"Sure," she muttered. Then she stopped, a confused expression on her face. "How did you find us?"

He smiled. "I tracked your energy here. We already knew that Don was heading to his brother's place because that's what he told us. However, once we got the report back that Darren was already dead, I knew Don would probably be here. I was pretty worried he wanted to take you out, so you couldn't interfere with his life anymore."

"It's so sad to think that he's ending up like this," she whispered.

"It's sad, but it's not your fault. However, I do have some good news for you." He looked over at Gage. "You want to tell her?"

Gage smiled at her and announced, "We found your sister. She's alive, and actually … she's a nurse and living right here in town."

Sadie stared at him in shock. "Really?"

He nodded. "For all intents and purposes, though it's a little early to be sure yet, she seems to be completely normal."

Sadie immediately burst into tears and burrowed her head tightly against Morrison's chest.

When she finally calmed down enough, he added, "Come on. I'm taking you home." But first she had to go to the police station and give her statement. So, by the time she collapsed onto her couch in her own apartment, she stared up at Morrison, exhausted. "I'm just done."

"That's why you're going straight to bed," he suggested.

"What will you do?"

"I'll stay here for the night, and we'll reassess in the morning."

She nodded, not sure what to say to that. She didn't want to say goodbye. Hell, she didn't want to say anything to him right now, except to have him stay with her. "Please stay. You've got to be as tired as I am."

"Maybe not quite as tired, but I'm definitely wiped," he admitted, with a smile. "Now get to bed, and we'll pick this up in the morning."

She stumbled off to bed, and, while he watched, she was out cold in a matter of minutes.

# CHAPTER 17

SADIE WOKE EARLY the next morning, staring around her room. Feeling a weight beside her, she rolled over to see Morrison stretched out beside her, atop the covers, wearing only jeans, seemingly sound asleep. She smiled, then gently stroked his cheek. "How come you're out here in the cold and not under the covers?" she whispered.

He opened one eye, looked at her, and explained a bit sheepishly, "Last night you were having nightmares, so that's why I'm here, and also why I'm not under the covers."

"Ah," she muttered, her hand falling away. She stared up at the ceiling for a long moment. "I wonder how long it will take before the nightmares ease up."

"It won't take long," he replied. "You have a lot of good people around you, and I'm sure you'll get through this just fine."

"It doesn't feel like it just yet," she noted. "It feels shitty all around."

"Of course it does. You found two siblings, lost one before you even had a chance to meet him, and the other one? Well, he's obviously been through so much that part of him is badly broken."

"I think he must have been sexually abused," she shared, turning to look at Morrison, "when he was younger, you know? All of them probably. His story was confusing, and

I'm not sure that we'll ever get the whole story."

"I'm not sure he's capable of telling the whole story, but maybe, over time, as he heals, with some proper care in a stable environment, he might make measurable improvements."

She didn't know what to say to that, but she looked at him and smiled. "You're trying to be optimistic for me, and I appreciate that."

He burst out laughing, as he propped himself up on his elbow. "Trying to be positive is one thing," he murmured. "But I think, in your brother's case, there has been a lot of trauma in his life; and, with any luck, he can get the help he needs. As far as the shootings and all the victims, a lot of them will be put on Darren's plate. We don't know whether he did it, or his brother, but it won't matter in the eyes of the law. Either way, your brother Don is not fit to stand trial any time soon, if ever, and that's where it ends."

"Right, and he'll be in therapy a long time, won't he?"

"He'll be a permanent resident in a psychiatric hospital, trying to get help. I don't know that he'll ever be well enough to get out. So, we need to prepare ourselves for that possibility."

"Yes, and I hate to say it, but a part of me would be relieved if that were the case. He's scary right now."

"He is, especially when he flips back and forth between personalities, and you don't know just what's going on. In fact, he may have more than just the two known personalities."

"That's something I've never experienced before," she whispered.

"Hey, neither have I. Not many of us have ever seen that, and it's not that common, and yet it's not considered uncommon either," Morrison shared. "It's just nothing we've seen until now."

She smiled. "So, what are your plans?"

"I'm taking some time off," he shared, rolling over on his back. "I've met this woman, and I know she's been having a tough time, so I thought maybe I would spend a few days with her and ensure she'll be okay."

"I can tell you right now that she'll be okay," she declared. "It takes a lot more than that to knock her for a loop."

"It did seem to me that she was pretty resilient," he confirmed, with a chuckle. "On the other hand, she got the stuffing knocked out of her a couple times, with events well beyond her control."

"Absolutely," she agreed, rolling over and smiling up at him. "Besides, that same woman very much wants to know if there's a relationship in the offing here, and, if there is, just how she should go about getting there."

"Well now," he began, looking at her with a twinkle in his eyes, "that depends on what kind of relationship she wants."

"We can start with one of mutual appreciation and affection, then move into some hot and steamy sex," she suggested, as she leaned over and kissed him.

"I really like the last part."

"What's wrong with the first part?" she asked, frowning at him.

He burst out laughing, pulled her atop him. "Somehow I'm thinking you'll probably want me to go shave first to avoid whisker burns."

"That's fine. Go shave if you prefer. I'm not going anywhere today, and neither are you," she stated, lifting her head to stare at him inquisitively.

"No, I'm here for a couple days at least, if that's okay with you."

"It's absolutely okay with me," she confirmed, "and then I might talk to Terkel."

"Oh? What about Terk?"

"He mentioned something about spending some time at his place to learn about this stuff," she reminded him. "I need to know an awful lot more, so I'm thinking I'll take him up on the offer."

"I agree," he said. "Opportunities like that don't come along very often."

"I got that impression," she noted, smiling at him as she kissed him gently on the chin. "So maybe, just maybe, I should do that. Where will you be?"

"I have a place a county over," he added, with a smile. "Close to but not living in the castle though." At the word *castle*, her eyes widened, and he nodded. "Their compound is located on the site of an old castle, which they've updated into some very cool headquarters," he noted, "and I have a pretty nice little country home not too far away. Not that I've told them about it. Although I'm sure Terk already knows."

"That's perfect," she declared. "I would suggest that I stay with you, but, you know, that castle just might win out."

He chuckled. "You can always split your time between both," he suggested, "but a word of warning. A lot of kids are at the castle."

"Kids," she repeated, her eyebrows raised.

"Lots of kids, nearly all of them under two years of age."

Her eyes widened again, and she started to laugh. "Oh,

Lord, I don't know if I'm up for that."

"Exactly. Take some time and figure out just what it is you want to do, with no pressure from anyone else, myself included. You haven't had two seconds to yourself since your mom died, so maybe a holiday, a break, a chance to reassess what you want in life is in order."

"I will take you up on that," she agreed, "but one of the things that I would like to do is take some time to assess whether or not we have something together."

"Ah, I would say from my perspective that no assessment is required on that point," he declared. "I absolutely think we have something special, and it just becomes a matter of whether you want to do the work for a relationship or not."

"They are work, aren't they?"

"Absolutely they are, no matter how well things go," he stated. "Compromises are required."

"*Hmm.* I'm not sure I'm into compromise just now."

He chuckled. "I'm starting to see a whole lot more to you than I saw before."

"Absolutely there is more," she said, chuckling. "What there is right now is somebody who would very much like you to kiss her."

As his eyebrows shot up, a smile lifted the corners of his mouth, and he whispered as he flipped her over and under him. "Your every wish is my command."

"Oh, I don't think so just yet," she teased, as she wiggled beneath him. "But maybe, just maybe, we'll get there."

He lowered his head and kissed her.

The kiss knocked her socks off, if she'd been wearing any. That kiss held such a smooth heat, a sense of rightness, almost as if puzzle pieces in her life fell into place, and she was stunned. When he lifted his head, she stared up at him, her eyes wide, and whispered, "Wow."

He nodded. "Wow is right, but then isn't that how it's supposed to be?" he asked, his nose gently nudging back and forth against hers. "There should definitely be a wow factor."

"I'm glad to hear that," she whispered, as she kissed him again and then again. Finally he lowered his head, putting her out of her misery, with a deep kiss of heat and longing, then proceeded to raise her blood pressure to a point that she could barely even control her cries and her squirms as she wriggled beneath him. "Damn it," she muttered, "you have way-too-many clothes on."

He ignored that comment as he slowly caressed and explored every inch of her, carefully stopping at all the interesting places, until she pleaded with him to stop teasing. He chuckled, hopped off the bed, and quickly stripped down, then tossed her skimpy excuse for a nightie onto the floor beside him.

She smiled, then opened her arms for him. "You know I'm totally okay with everything that happened, if the result was meeting you."

And, with a nod and a big smile, he slowly climbed her body, slid inside, and rested at the heart of her. He grabbed her hands, pulled them up over her head until she was arched beneath him, and whispered, "Ditto."

Then he slowly started to move. She was crying out within minutes, her body in an agony of delight and torment, when she suddenly exploded beneath him, and it took only a couple more plunges on his part before he joined her. He collapsed beside her, a smile on his face, and whispered, "I guess maybe you don't have to worry about the whisker burns after all."

She chuckled. "How about you go shave, and we will try

it all over again? Let's see which is better."

"I was thinking about maybe a shower with you," he offered, mischief in his eyes.

"Oh, I like that idea," she said in delight.

He turned his head and waited a beat. "Maybe in a minute though."

"Why?" she asked.

"I think you killed me."

She chuckled. "If I killed you, you'll have to work up some endurance." He raised an eyebrow and looked at her, as she shrugged. "It's been a long time for me, so I just might be a little hungry." She slid a hand over his big, warm chest. "Like a lot hungry." She leaned over and kissed him, wrapping her arms around him, then her thighs, as she rolled him onto his back and mounted him.

He shuddered beneath her and whispered, "I always did like a gal with a big appetite."

She burst out laughing and proceeded to carry them both back to their place of pure joy.

# EPILOGUE

T ERK LOOKED UP with interest as the newcomers arrived at the dining room table. He recognized the appetite for a fulfilling relationship and the cementing of their energy-worker bond, and he nodded. "Welcome," he greeted them. "Your rooms are ready, whenever you want to take your luggage up. If you're staying here, that is, as I understand Morrison has a place close by."

Sadie sat down across from Terk and reached out for a handshake, as she smiled. "Thank you."

He gave her a gentle smile in return, shaking her hand. "What are you thanking me for?" he asked, amusement rippling through his tone.

"I don't know whether it should be for giving me a place to stay, for the support I've needed, for the help with my brothers, or for tossing Morrison in my direction. Definitely for all of those things."

"For all that, you are welcome. Besides you have talents that could use some honing and ones we want to learn more about, so it's a good trade-off.

She realized for the first time that there really was a profound sense of connection and community here. But she would learn more, and she would understand more.

Just then Terk's phone rang. He groaned as he reached for his phone and asked, "Jonas, what's up?"

"I need two men right now," he snapped, "as in today."

"Depends on where you are."

"I'm in London, and I need somebody right now."

"As in twenty minutes from now?"

"Preferably ten minutes from now," he added urgently. "I have one guy here who told me to call you to get backup, but I don't know if he's one of yours or not."

"Who is it?" Terk asked curiously, as he looked around the dining room table, knowing that most of his men were here, though a few were still off on jobs.

"His name is Wallace."

At that Terk stiffened. "Wallace Cremayne?"

Muffled voices came from the other end of the call, and a new voice came on board. "Hey, Terk. Wallace here. Jonas has a problem."

"Jonas always has a problem," Terk noted. "What are you doing there?"

"I came over because they wanted to talk to me about bringing up a unit similar to what you were doing for the CIA," he explained. "They figured that you were too big and too government-shy to want to do it."

"So, they contacted you?" Terk asked in amusement. "I guess they didn't look into your history too much."

"Nope, they sure didn't, but, while we were here, one of the researchers that they were also trying to hire has disappeared."

At that, Terk closed his eyes, pinched the bridge of his nose, and got straight to the point. "Don't tell me it's Amy."

"Yeah, it's Amy," Wallace confirmed. "Amy Connelly. I'm going after her, but I don't know what we'll need. Jonas is asking for two backups, but, honest to God, if I even had one, I would be happy."

More chatter came in the background, and then Riff joined the call.

"Hey, Terk. I'm here in London already, so I can handle this. You guys enjoy setting up home for the latest newcomers." And, with that, Riff was gone, and the call ended.

Terk stared down at the phone and then looked at the others gathered at the table with him. "That was interesting. Riff's in London, where Wallace was doing something for Jonas, but apparently Amy's disappeared, and we need all hands on deck for this one."

"Amy?" Several of the women looked at each other, then back at Terk.

He nodded. "Somebody I knew as a kid. You guys probably don't know her, but Merk and I do. Damn, I'll need to tell Merk. If Levi's got anybody to help, maybe we can get him to pinch-hit, as needed." Then he frowned and tapped the table, as precog images started filtering through his brain. "Well, shit, she's been kidnapped, and they want her to do research for them, but I don't know who it is. I'm definitely feeling …" Then he frowned. "I feel as if Asia's coming into this somehow."

"From London to Asia?" Celia asked.

He shrugged. "Or big money, as in China maybe? I don't know." Terk shook his head. "But they need help, and we need to help them now."

This concludes Book 13 of Terk's Guardians: Morrison.
Read about Wallace: Terk's Guardians, Book 14

# Terk's Guardians: Wallace (Book #14)

He wasn't sure why he'd answered Jonas's call to discuss setting up a unit akin to Terk's remarkable team—perhaps it was curiosity, or something more. But as soon as he lands, he's thrust into a crisis: one of the new research hires has vanished, and Jonas fears the worst. Then he hears the name…

Amy, an old friend of Terk's, had been swept into peril without warning. Captured, with no clue as to where she was, why she was taken, or by whom. She managed to send a desperate message to Terk, and only when she connected with him mentally did her panic transform into steely determination. Whoever was behind this would pay. She wasn't alone anymore. She had powerful allies. Allies who, even now, were racing to her aid… she hoped.

For Wallace, finding Amy became an urgent mission, and ensuring her safe return was a close second. But what seemed like a straightforward rescue quickly spirals into a tangled web of danger and intrigue. Amidst the chaos, an unexpected connection sparks between them, adding a layer of complexity to their perilous journey and the stakes become more personal than ever.

Find Book 14 here!

To find out more visit Dale Mayer's website.

https://geni.us/DMSWallace

# Author's Note

Thank you for reading Morrison: Terk's Guardians, Book 13! If you enjoyed the book, please take a moment and leave a short review.

Dear reader,

I love to hear from readers, and you can contact me at my website: www.dalemayer.com or at my Facebook author page. To be informed of new releases and special offers, sign up for my newsletter or follow me on BookBub. And if you are interested in joining Dale Mayer's Reader Group, here is the Facebook sign up page.
http://geni.us/DaleMayerFBGroup

Cheers,
Dale Mayer

# About the Author

Dale Mayer is a *USA Today* best-selling author, best known for her SEALs military romances, her Psychic Visions series, and her Lovely Lethal Garden cozy series. Her contemporary romances are raw and full of passion and emotion (Broken But ... Mending, Hathaway House series). Her thrillers will keep you guessing (Kate Morgan, By Death series), and her romantic comedies will keep you giggling (*It's a Dog's Life*, a stand-alone novella; and the Broken Protocols series, starring Charming Marvin, the cat).

Dale honors the stories that come to her—and some of them are crazy, break all the rules and cross multiple genres!

To go with her fiction, she also writes nonfiction in many different fields, with books available on résumé writing, companion gardening, and the US mortgage system. All her books are available in print and ebook format.

## Connect with Dale Mayer Online

*Dale's Website – www.dalemayer.com*
*Twitter – @DaleMayer*
*Facebook Page – geni.us/DaleMayerFBFanPage*
*Facebook Group – geni.us/DaleMayerFBGroup*
*BookBub – geni.us/DaleMayerBookbub*
*Instagram – geni.us/DaleMayerInstagram*
*Goodreads – geni.us/DaleMayerGoodreads*
*Newsletter – geni.us/DaleNews*

www.ingramcontent.com/pod-product-compliance
Lightning Source LLC
Chambersburg PA
CBHW070628170726
48291CB00003B/925